"I THOUGHT
SMART FEM   EM
TERRIBLY L

"I don't unders
breath was com   ... ..e was so close that
her body yearned to touch him.

"Maybe," he said, his eyes glinting, "maybe you'll
understand this." And, his hands sliding down to
grip her waist, he lifted her bodily to meet his
kiss. There was no way she could refuse him, no
way to keep her body from responding to his.

Nothing mattered but the warm embrace of his
arms, pinning her body against his, her breasts
crushed against his chest, his mouth heavy on
hers. She forgot everything except the rising
desire to join herself with him, to belong to
him . . .

NINA COOMBS was raised in Ohio. In addition to raising five children, she managed to earn a Ph.D. in Eng-
lish literature. As she says, "I write regularly, almost
like I eat and sleep. If I don't write, I don't feel well.
Aside from writing, the big loves in my life are horses,
Montana, and the man who first took me there."

Dear Reader:

Signet has always been known for its consistently fine individual romances, and now we are proud to introduce a provocative new line of contemporary romances, RAPTURE ROMANCE. While maintaining our high editorial standards, RAPTURE ROMANCE will explore all the possibilities that exist when today's men and women fall in love. Mutual respect, gentle affection, raging passion, tormenting jealousy, overwhelming desire, and finally, pure rapture—the moods of romance will be vividly presented in the kind of sensual, yet always tasteful detail that makes a fantasy real. We are very enthusiastic about RAPTURE ROMANCE, and we hope that you will enjoy reading these novels as much as we enjoy finding and publishing them for you!

In fact, please let us know what you do think—we love to hear from our readers, and what you tell us about your likes and dislikes is taken seriously. We have enclosed a questionnaire with some of our own queries at the back of this book. Please take a few minutes to fill it out, or if you prefer, write us directly at the address below.

And don't forget that your favorite RAPTURE ROMANCE authors need your encouragement; although we can't give out addresses, we will be happy to forward any mail.

We look forward to hearing from you!

Robin Grunder
RAPTURE ROMANCE
New American Library
1633 Broadway
New York, NY 10019

LOVE SO FEARFUL

by
Nina Coombs

RAPTURE ROMANCE
NEW AMERICAN LIBRARY
TIMES MIRROR
PUBLISHED BY
THE NEW AMERICAN LIBRARY
OF CANADA LIMITED

For those who find
love fearful
yet still pursue it

PUBLISHER'S NOTE

This novel is a work of fiction. Names, characters, places, and incidents are either the product of the author's imagination or are used fictitiously, and any resemblance to actual persons, living or dead, events, or locales is entirely coincidental.

NAL BOOKS ARE AVAILABLE AT QUANTITY DISCOUNTS WHEN USED TO PROMOTE PRODUCTS OR SERVICES. FOR INFORMATION PLEASE WRITE TO PREMIUM MARKETING DIVISION, THE NEW AMERICAN LIBRARY, INC., 1633 BROADWAY, NEW YORK, NEW YORK 10019.

First Printing, January, 1983

2 3 4 5 6 7 8 9

SIGNET, SIGNET CLASSICS, MENTOR, PLUME, MERIDIAN and NAL BOOKS are published in Canada by The New American Library of Canada, Limited, Scarborough, Ontario
PRINTED IN CANADA
COVER PRINTED IN U.S.A.

Chapter One

❦

Megan Ryan pushed her new Stetson to the back of her long auburn hair and surveyed herself in the dressing-room mirror. The new plaid shirt clinging to her body did not make her look any more businesslike, but at least she would not arrive at the ranch looking like some stupid city girl. She was lucky to get this job, very lucky, she told herself. Coming west had been an adventure in itself, and now she was going to start her job as resident veterinarian at the Rocking D, outside Miles City, Montana.

After graduating from veterinary college she had worked in several pet hospitals near Cleveland, Ohio, but Megan was a country girl at heart, born and raised on a farm, and horses were her first love. Not surprisingly, few horses found their way to pet hospitals. The farm was gone, sold after her parents' death, the money barely sufficing to pay off the debts. She had no ties in Ohio, no ties anywhere. So she had applied for the Montana job with a free heart. She had to admit that getting it had been a surprise. But the prospect of playing doctor to a ranch full of horses sounded like sheer heaven.

Megan's eyes—the velvet brown of pansies—slid over the rest of her figure, the blue jeans molding nicely rounded hips, the new boots on her small feet. She might be little, she thought, but five feet three inches could be tough. She had proved that more than once through the years.

She took in the belt around her slim waist one more notch and picked up the pile of clothes she had worn into the store. "These will be fine," she told the waiting clerk, who had already been asked for advice about what the ordinary person hereabouts wore. "If you'll just snip off the tags," continued Megan with a smile, "I'll wear them."

Actually, aside from the boots, her new clothes were not much different from some of those she had packed. This shopping trip had just given her a chance to relax a little before she met her new boss. His directions to the Rocking D had been quite explicit, and Megan anticipated no trouble in finding it.

She took up her packages, and, with another smile for the clerk, returned once more to the street. The sun was high in a brilliant blue sky, and Megan squinted up at it with all the wonder of an Easterner for whom gray skies are normal. Then she shook herself briskly and started off toward the side street where she had parked the car. Her steps grew faster as she realized that she had spent longer than she meant to in the shop. She didn't want to begin her stay in this city by getting a parking ticket.

She rounded the corner almost at a run and slammed into a hard male chest. "Easy there, young'un," drawled the big cowboy whose rough hands on her shoulders were steadying her. For the barest second Megan stood still, conscious of the comfortable smell of leather and horses which emanated from the man. Then she raised her gaze and met a pair of flashing blue eyes in a rugged bronzed face. The smile he gave her was rueful as his eyes traveled farther down her body. "Sorry about that, miss. You ain't no young'un. That's for sure."

His eyes were frankly appraising, and Megan stiffened. Cowboys, she supposed, were no different from other men. Men had found her attractive during her years in school, but they had invariably been of two kinds: those who wanted an enjoyable fling—a roll in the hay, as this cowboy might say—and those who, becoming serious, expected her to give up her career. So far Megan had found no man worth giving up what she had worked so hard for. Nor, she had told herself, did she ever intend to love so selfish a person. She did want love, of course, but a long-lasting, nourishing kind, not the sort that limited and confined. All this raced through her mind as she gazed into this attractive man's eyes.

"Excuse me," she said in the coldest voice she could manage, meanwhile extricating herself from his grasp.

He was not put off. "What for? I was in your way. Say, you're new in town, aren't you?"

"Yes." The answer popped out of its own volition, and she was instantly angry with herself. She had a job to do, and it didn't include flirting with passing cowboys.

"What's your name?" he asked, his deep voice a caress, his eyes now clearly admiring.

Glaring, Megan stepped around him, her knuckles tightening on her package. She didn't like this man. He was too blatantly male, the kind that women run after. No doubt he expected her to throw herself at his feet, she thought crossly as she stamped away, the heels of her new boots clattering on the pavement.

"Hey, wait," he called, amusement in his voice. "Don't go off mad."

But Megan ignored this, and fortunately he did not follow her. Her mouth tightened grimly as she climbed into the little cream-colored VW Bug that had carried her across the country. If he had tried anything, she told herself, he would have been good and sorry.

She tossed the package in the back and forced herself to take slow deep breaths. Her heart was pounding, and her body was flushed with a sudden heat not caused by the sun. Why did a man like that affect her so, she wondered, when she had always despised his type? She closed her eyes briefly, willing herself to see a cool blue lake, her usual procedure for calming herself. But this time it didn't work. Instead of the lake she was used to imagining, her mind presented her with a picture of the cowboy. That picture, in spite of the fact that she had only seen him once, was surprisingly complete. The rugged sun-bronzed face was topped by unruly black hair curling out from under a battered dusty Stetson. His nose was bold and his chin strong. His forehead carried a diagonal scar, she realized now as his features came back to her. The chest into which she had so abruptly run was covered by a plaid shirt, slightly damp, she recalled, frowning as the memory of crisp black chest hair protruding from above the top button came back to her. The picture of his bottom half was less clear, but her hands had felt only hard male muscle in their brief contact with his midsection, and the blood flooded to her face at the sharp recall of the hard thrust of his thighs against her own during their collision.

Megan opened her eyes with a start and shook her head crossly. She was being ridiculous. Far better to be thinking about her new job. No doubt Montana was full of big virile cowboys. She would get used to them. She took out her directions and concentrated.

About half an hour later Megan drove the little Bug under a big wooden Rocking D. So far so good, she told herself as the little car bumped over the metal cattle guard. Driving slowly along the somewhat rutted lane, she eyed the ranch as it unfolded before her. It was a good-sized spread, she thought, glancing off into the prairie at a herd of cattle grazing nearby. She already knew it was a working ranch and that there would be cattle to care for, but it was the horses that she looked forward to—strong, solid, friendly horses.

The years of her youth had been graced by horses. To her, they were better friends than dogs. And here she would be caring for many. The ad had made it plain that horses would be the main part of her job. Megan's generous lips parted in a smile. She could hardly wait to get to them!

She followed the rutted lane past the ranch house, rather old-fashioned, but comfortable-looking, and down to the stables. The place looked weatherbeaten, but she decided that was only natural. After all, it was a working ranch.

She stopped the car and straightened her shoulders. What a time to get an attack of nerves, she thought wryly. She hadn't been conscious of nervousness before this. After all, it wasn't likely that Mr. Dutton would let someone come clear across country if he didn't mean to keep them on.

She pushed open the little car's door and stepped out, settling her new Stetson more firmly on her head. Now to find Mr. Dutton. She moved toward the door of what looked like the tack room, wondering what her new boss would look like. Knocking briskly, she called out, "Anyone around?"

"In here," came the gruff reply.

Megan pushed open the door and stepped inside. The room was dim after the bright sunshine outside, and she blinked rapidly, trying to adjust her eyes to the darkness.

"Yes, miss?" The gruff voice seemed slightly softened. "You lookin' for someone?"

Megan nodded, her eyes now making out the grizzled man sitting in the corner. "Yes, I'm looking for the owner."

"The boss ain't back yet," said the old hand, allowing his eyes to travel over her. "Did he know you was coming?"

"Yes," said Megan, wondering if all Western men looked at women in this frankly assessing fashion. "But he didn't know when to expect me."

A brown work-roughened hand reached up to scratch his head. "That don't sound like the boss. He likes 'em prompt."

Megan colored. "I think you've made some kind of mistake," she said crisply. "I'm Megan Ryan, the new vet."

"The what?" The cowhand got to his feet and stood staring at her. "You ain't! You can't be!"

Megan put down a surge of irritation. "Please, Mr.—"

"Pete Greeves," he said. "Call me Pete."

"Please, Mr. Greeves, I assure you that I am Megan Ryan and I am the new vet. Mr. Dutton expected me sometime this week. Here." She opened her purse. "I have his letter."

"Don't need that," Pete replied, aiming a stream of tobacco at an unsuspecting fly. "Know your name and your record." Shrewd gray eyes met hers. "Helped to pick you out myself. But I didn't expect no China doll. Thought you'd be a big strapping Irish lass."

Megan's irritation vanished. "I am Irish, Mr.

Greeves. And in spite of my small size I'm quite capable." She gave him a warm smile. "Good things come in small packages, you know."

Pete's wrinkled face lit up with a mischievous grin. "You've already convinced this old Irishman," he said. "I never could resist a pretty lass. And you got good credentials. I seen 'em." He shook his head. "But damned if you don't look like you'd break if a man so much as touched you."

Megan laughed. "I assure you, Pete, I'm tough as nails. You'll see."

Pete nodded. "It's the boss I'm thinking about now. He wasn't none too strong on hiring a woman." His weatherbeaten face puckered in a frown. "Fact, he was against it. Was me persuaded him." He sighed. "An' it's me gonna get cussed out."

"That's silly," Megan said, wishing this boss were there. "What difference does my size make?"

"Them horses is big," Pete said. "You kin ride, can't you?"

Megan's laughter rang out, clear and low. "Since I was five, Pete. Horses are my first love. That's why I applied for this job."

"Of course." He picked up an ancient Stetson and clapped it on his head. "It's just—you look so delicate like, even in that rig. Where's your stuff? Might as well get you settled in afore Bart gets back," he added with a grin.

"My car's right out there," Megan replied. "You don't think he'll send me away, do you?" she asked anxiously as she followed him outside. "I mean, I came all the way from Ohio."

Pete shrugged. "Can't make no promises where the boss's concerned," he said. "But he's a fair man."

Megan, opening the car door, gave him a dry look.

"What a consolation that is!" She pulled out a suitcase and set it on the ground.

Pete chuckled. "Let me give you a piece of advice, little lady. Don't come on to the boss with that snooty tone. He'll soon put you in your place."

"Really!" Megan was seriously beginning to doubt the wisdom of having taken this job, but she continued to pull cases from the car.

"The boss gets a little testy now and then," Pete said, cheerfully gathering up bags. "But he's got his reasons. Being a world champion saddle-bronc rider ain't no piece of cake, ya know. Hitting the dust ain't like falling into no featherbed. Bones get broke that way."

Following him across the yard with a suitcase in each hand, Megan sighed. She would have to get a job with a man who was impossible to please.

"This here's gonna be your office," said Pete, pushing through the door at the other side of the tack room. "It's kind of dusty now."

Megan's suitcases dropped from her hands. Kind of! The room was festooned with cobwebs, like a scene from a horror movie, she thought, and the dust on the floor must be almost an inch deep.

"I meant to clean it up," said Pete apologetically. "But I been busy." He moved on, leaving a trail of footprints in the dust. "There's another room over here." He indicated an open doorway. "Sort of thought she'd sleep here." He looked at her and shook his head again. "Like I told you, I thought you'd be a big strapping lass."

"It's all right," Megan said, trying to sound as if this was what she had expected. Pete set the suitcase on the cot, raising a cloud of dust that set her coughing. When she could stop, she asked, "When can I find a broom and a pail and scrub brush?"

"I'll get ya some," said Pete. "Right away."

"And better not bring in anything else," Megan called after him. "Not till I get this cleaned." She took off her new Stetson and looked around. There wasn't a clean spot in the room to put it down in. With another sigh, she carried it back to the tack room and hung it on an empty peg. Then she rolled up her sleeves and set to work.

Two hours later Megan straightened wearily. Her new shirt was stuck to her back. The rooms were hot and stuffy, and even the two little windows that had had finally forced open at the cost of a broken fingernail didn't let in much air. Her hair was plastered to her neck, the jeans felt as if she'd been swimming in them, and her new boots hurt. This job was not at all what she had bargained for. She wiped at the perspiration on her forehead, leaving another smudge of dust on her cheek.

At least the office was shaping up, she told herself. Now for the bedroom. She would carry the mattress out to air in the sun. No matter how tired she was she could not consider sleeping on that filthy thing. With a weary sigh she shifted the suitcases onto the floor. She would have to ask Pete for some linen. Surely the job didn't entail sleeping without sheets.

For a moment she surveyed the offending mattress. Even the dust didn't hide several holes in the ticking. After his comments, she didn't intend to ask Pete for help. She took the mattress from one end and rolled it up. Thin and lumpy as it was, it was still too thick to get her arms around it. With an exasperated groan she let it fall back on the protesting springs. She would have to drag it outside. There was no other way. And she might as well do it now. Megan grabbed it by one end and jerked it to the floor.

Thank God, she had found the rudiments of a bathroom in a little niche off the so-called bedroom— only a toilet, a cracked sink, and a tin-walled shower stall, but at least she could get clean there. If she ever finished grubbing through this dust and dirt.

By dint of much maneuvering she finally reached the outside, trailing the offending mattress behind her. With a muffled exclamation of annoyance she looked around. There must be some place clean around here. Finally her eye lit on the Bug. She had had it washed yesterday. She would use the top of it! She wrestled the mattress across the intervening space to the car. It took a lot of huffing and puffing, but she finally got the wretched thing draped across the hood and stood back, hands on hips, resting for a precious moment before she returned to battle the dust.

Megan was not a cursing woman, but the sight of the disreputable mattress, which in the sunlight looked even worse, got under her skin. How could a man expect anyone, male or female, to live in that filth? With a muffled curse she spun on her boot heel. The rest of the dirt awaited her—and she meant to conquer it.

"Oh!" Again Megan collided with a male chest. And she didn't need the scent of horses and leather to tell her that this was the same cowboy she had seen in town. Her patience worn thin by her fatigue, she backed away a step and glared up at him. "What are you doing here?" she snapped.

"That," said the cowboy with a frown, "is exactly what I want to ask you."

"If it's any of your business," she retorted. "I happen to work here."

"Since when—"

"Since Mr. Dutton hired me," she replied.

"Mr. Dutton," he repeated, one eyebrow lifting. "So Mr. Dutton hired you."

Megan nodded. "That's exactly what I said. Now if you'll just get out of my way I'll get back to work."

"What kind of work? Are you a cleaning lady?" She didn't miss the trace of amusement in his voice.

"I happen to be the Rocking D's new vet," she said sharply.

"My new *what*?" he cried. The blue eyes turned suddenly cold, piercing her with a sharp stare.

It was Megan's turn to stare. "Did—did you say *your*?"

"I did," he replied. "I'm Bart Dutton. And you're really—"

"Megan Ryan. I'm sorry, Mr. Dutton. I had no idea. I thought—" She smiled ruefully, wishing he wouldn't look at her like that. "I'm hot and tired. And crabby, I'm afraid."

He nodded. "What are you doing with that thing?"

"I'm airing my mattress," Megan said calmly. "I've just about got the room done."

For a long moment Bart Dutton stared at her, and she wondered if he even heard her. "Mr. Dutton."

"The name's Bart," he said absently. "But you don't belong here. I told Pete getting a woman was a mistake, but the old fool hung on to the idea. Brighten up the place, he said. Be good for morale."

Megan's temper, never well under control, threatened to rise again. "I am a veterinarian, Mr. Dutton, not a decoration. If you want to brighten up the place," she said crisply, "you'd better try something else. I'm going to be busy taking care of horses."

"Not mine," he replied.

"What do you mean, not yours?" she demanded, wishing herself back in Ohio where people behaved decently.

"Just what I said. You're only a snip of a thing."

As he was looking down at her from his six-foot height, she could hardly refute that, but she tried for dignity as she replied. "My size does not have anything to do with my efficiency on the job. I take it you don't expect me to *lift* the horses."

Her sarcasm made little impression on him, though she saw one dark eyebrow lift momentarily. "Of course not. But this job takes stamina."

"I *have* stamina," Megan asserted.

"You?" His eyes were frankly disbelieving. "You look like you've never lifted a finger in your life."

Since she had just spent a long weary time cleaning a room not fit for a pig, and she knew she was dirty and dusty, her temper snapped. "I don't care what I look like," Megan cried. This man was driving her crazy. "I can do the job as well as any man!"

He pushed his Stetson back, a lock of black hair falling over his forehead. "Maybe you can handle the mares," he said. "Even an occasional sick steer. But I just got a new stallion, Diablo. And he's rightly named. He's the meanest devil I've ever seen. But I'll tame him."

Megan frowned. "How does this horse behave?"

Bart shook his head. "You must be crazy, girl. How does he behave? I'll tell you. It's not enough that he bucks cowboys off. Saddle broncs are supposed to do that. But this crazy brute thinks he's a bull and tries to stomp them. Even the rodeos don't want him, and the stock companies think he's too mean to have around. But he's got great lines. That's why I bought him. I mean to breed him." A hard look came into his eyes. "And I'll tame him."

"Do you know anything about the background of this horse? When did he go sour?"

Bart shrugged. "Who the hell knows? I'm going to

breed the horse, not marry him," he cried in exasperation.

"He's probably been mistreated," Megan continued in the same line of thought. "A little kindness might bring him around."

Bart Dutton snorted. "A little kindness! You *are* crazy. What that horse needs is a heavy hand. A real heavy hand."

Megan could only glare at him. "Just like a man. Handle everything with power. Make everyone give in."

Bart nodded. "Men are stronger than women. And smarter than horses."

Megan's exclamation of disgust was barely repressed, and his grin told her he had heard it.

"Animals," she said, "are not like people. Usually they have good reason for their viciousness."

He didn't bother to reply to this as once more his eyes surveyed her thoughtfully. "Okay, you can stay. For a month. On probation."

Megan's elation was short-lived. Probation! But then common sense came to the fore. And her Irish stubbornness. She was not the kind to give in. Bart Dutton would find that out.

"There's one thing, though," he added, his lips tightening in a grim line. "None of your fancy theories about kindness. That stallion's off limits unless he's really sick. Agreed?"

"Agreed." The word came reluctantly, but Megan knew she had to say it. She felt absolutely wilted. The heat was getting to her, and she wiped at her forehead with a dirty hand. "And now if I can just get on with my cleaning—"

Bart Dutton shook his head. "Where's your stuff?"

"Some's in the car, some's in there—in my room." She said the word with a shiver of distaste.

"You're not sleeping out here," he said brusquely. "So just forget it. You'll take one of the bedrooms in the house." He frowned as he pushed aside the mattress and opened the car door. "I'll show you a room and then send someone for the rest of your stuff. Wait'll I get that Pete," he muttered. "I'll give the old devil an earful."

Megan considered protesting, but when she thought about spending the night in that horrible little room, really thought about it, she decided to remain silent. She picked up two cases and followed him up the track to the house.

The room he gave her was bright and sunny, with large windows and an adjoining bath. Megan tried to repress a sigh of relief at the sight ot it. "Thank you, Mr. Dutton," she said with a sincerity that was quite heartfelt.

"Better call me Bart," he said. "We aren't that formal here. You'll eat at the house, too. Mrs. Grean's an excellent cook. Just tell her what you want."

"That's hardly necessary," Megan began. "I can cook for myself."

The smile he gave her then was grim. "Not in Mrs. Grean's kitchen. She's the best cook in the county, and if you go messing around in her kitchen she'll be gone quicker than a rattler can strike." He raised a warning finger. "And so will you. Understand?"

Megan nodded. "I understand, Mr. Dutton."

"Bart," he reminded her. He glanced at his watch. "Now I've got to run. Got to meet someone for dinner. I'll see you in the morning. Ask Mrs. Grean for anything you need."

"Thank you," Megan replied as she watched him cross the room, his long muscular legs stretching his dusty jeans taut.

So, Megan told herself as she opened a case and took out a change of clothing. That was Bart Dutton, her new boss. And a more attractive, more irritating man she had yet to find.

Chapter Two

❧

The song of a bird woke Megan in the morning. She stretched and was gratified to discover that she was not stiff and sore. She pushed back the covers and padded barefoot to the window. In the half-light before dawn, she smiled. It looked like the beginning of a beautiful day.

Minutes later she emerged from the bath and slipped into clean clothes. Hot and tired as she'd been yesterday, she hadn't forgotten to return to the stable, to get a grinning Pete to assign her a horse and saddle. She liked the little chestnut mare, Darling, that he had showed her and had asked to have the horse kept in the corral. "I mean to start my day with a ride," she had said, her face alive with the prospect.

Now, boots in hand, she crept out into the hall and down the stairs. Bart Dutton had not yet been home last night when she had fallen exhausted into bed, so she had no idea when he'd come in. And she certainly had no wish to start the day by meeting him.

In the kitchen she took her Stetson and jacket from

their pegs, noting that Bart's hat wasn't there. Maybe he slept with it, she thought with wry humor. Working for Bart Dutton was going to take some getting used to.

Coming into the stables from the cool morning air, she sniffed appreciatively. How she loved the good warm smell of horses! It meant home and safety to her.

She took a bridle down and went toward the stall that held the mare. A soft velvet nose poked out over the door, and Megan stroked it. "Good morning, girl. Want to go for a ride?"

The mare snorted and tossed her head as Megan slid the bridle onto it. "Easy girl," she said as she led the mare out. "We'll be out there soon." The mare was quickly saddled, so eager to go that she didn't even bother to blow out her belly against the cinch.

Megan inhaled deeply of the fresh morning air as she swung up into the saddle. Such beautiful country! She pointed the mare toward the east, where the sun was just peeping up over the prairie. A slight breeze ruffled her hair, making it flow out behind her, and Megan forgot her worries about the new job, forgot her irritation with Bart Dutton, forgot everything except the fresh feel of the wind in her face and the exhilarating rhythm of the horse between her knees. It had been so long since she'd been on horseback. She would do this every morning, she thought, jamming the Stetson down tighter on her head, letting her eyes sweep over the prairie before her.

Pale-pink fingers of light crept up over the horizon, mingling with streaks of orange, yellow, and rose. As she rode toward the sight the fingers of color widened and merged into a kaleidoscope of patterns that spread across the sky. Megan exhaled as the colors shifted and moved across the horizon. As far as she could see to

either side the lovely colors stretched, beautiful in their
varied changing hues.

She sighed. Back East you could never see a sunrise
like this. There were always tall buildings or short
ones, telephone wires, or some kind of obstruction.
Here the broad sweep of the prairie seemed endless.
There were buildings on it, of course, but they were
hidden by the nature of the land. Westeners knew that
the apparent flatness of the prairie was a deception. It
was really a great rolling expanse in which ranches,
and even whole towns, could disappear.

Megan rode down a slope to a small clump of cottonwoods and paused by the little creek that gurgled
there. To the east of her the light of the sun was
spreading across the sky in ever-widening bands of
color. Hooking a leg over the saddle horn, Megan let
herself relax and drink in the beauty around her. She
was going to like Montana. She was going to like it
a lot.

The horizon gradually brightened as the light spread.
The pungent smell of sagebrush tickled her nostrils as
she inhaled deeply. She let her eyes sweep out over the
horizon, glorying in the great expanse of it. So much
room, so much space. She sighed and realized suddenly
how loud the sound was. The silence of the prairie was
deep, deeper than any silence she had ever heard. A
feeling of peace stole over her. This was what people
needed. Space and silence. Again she inhaled deeply.

A small moving speck on the horizon caught her
eyes. Someone else was enjoying the morning. Megan
watched idly as the figure moved her way. Then, as it
drew closer, she felt a faint prickling in the fine hair
along the back of her neck. It couldn't be. Yet the
rider seemed familiar.

The horseman drew rapidly nearer. The light behind
him silhouetted the breadth of his shoulders, and her

breath caught in her throat. It couldn't be Bart Dutton. What was he doing out here at this time of day? She still couldn't see the man's face; the light behind him was too bright. The horse under him was mettlesome, though, fighting his rider. Maybe she should turn and ride back toward the ranch, just avoid this rider, whoever he might be. But no. She had to work with the man; it wouldn't do to let him think she was afraid of him.

She swung her leg down and hooked her boot back in the stirrup. The rider was close now, the horse dancing under him. He pulled up as he drew nearer.

"Well, well, what are you doing out here? I thought Eastern girls slept till noon."

For a wild second Megan wanted to dig her boots into the mare's sides and gallop for safety, but she squashed the feeling down with a surge of irritation. She didn't intend to let the man get to her. "Good morning, Mr. Dutton." She kept her tone noncommittal.

"The name's Bart," he said, smiling, those blue eyes intent on her.

"Good morning, Mr. Dutton," she repeated.

He shrugged, and Megan was again conscious of those broad muscular shoulders. "Good morning, Miss Ryan. I repeat my question. What are you doing out here?"

"I'm enjoying the sunrise." With difficulty she kept herself from returning his smile. He had a wide mouth with full, sensuous lips, she noticed for the first time. "I like to get up early," she continued. "Morning is the best time of day."

The mare moved restlessly under Megan; she was conscious of the stallion, too conscious. Megan patted the smooth silky neck to soothe her. She could understand the mare's skittishness, she thought wryly. She was feeling the impact of Bart Dutton's virile maleness. It put her nerves on edge and made breathing difficult.

As Bart edged the stallion closer, she saw his gloved hand tighten on the reins as the great horse fought him. Across the short distance that separated them she caught a whiff of leather and horses, a scent she already associated with Bart. Now it also carried a faint hint of sagebrush.

His free hand reached out toward her, resting lightly on her arm. "You're a skittish little thing," he said softly. "Whatever possessed you to come out here?"

Megan forced herself to remain calm, to ignore the hand that seemed to be burning into her arm. "I like horses, Mr. Dutton. In fact, I love them. That's why I took this job."

His hand stroked her arm gently, each touch sending a strange sensation through her taut body. "This is a long way to come for a job. A girl like you—all alone, clear across the country."

"I didn't mind." Megan's words were soft. She began to feel strangely relaxed, as if she were floating in a deep pool of warm water. His hand moved up her arm to touch her shoulder. "Your boyfriend must be crazy. To let a girl like you travel like that."

"I haven't any—" she began, almost mesmerized by that flashing smile.

"I can't believe that," he said, his voice warm.

It was then that the mare sidestepped nervously, pulling Megan away from that hand. For some moments all her attention was focused on bringing the horse under control. By the time she had achieved that, his spell was broken. How could she have let him talk to her like that, touch her like that? As if she were some, some . . . Color flooded her cheeks at the thought.

As he guided the stallion close again, Megan's control snapped. With a quick motion she turned the mare back toward the ranch and trotted off, throwing a clipped goodbye over her shoulder. Even at a distance she could feel his eyes burning into her back, and angrily she kicked the mare into a gallop. She heard the shout behind her, but she ignored it. A kind of panic swept over her, and without thinking she gave the chestnut her head. She only knew that she had to get away from the man whose touch had affected her so strangely.

Unbelievably she heard the pounding of another set of hooves behind her. He couldn't be following her. But he was! She turned her head to look back over her shoulder and saw that he was already almost beside her. At that instant the stallion lengthened his stride and Bart came thundering up beside her. Megan had time to give him only one glance of disgust before he leaned across and grabbed the reins. It took him only moments to pull the mare to a halt.

Megan turned on him angrily. "Who do you think you are?" she yelled, hoping her anger would serve as a defense against him. "Stopping my horse like that. You've no right!"

"I have every right," he said sharply, pushing his Stetson back. "You're a fool. A first-class fool."

"What are you talking about?" she demanded.

Bart Dutton glared at her in exasperation. "If you don't care about your own neck, at least think about the mare's."

Megan glared back. "You're talking sheer nonsense," she snapped. "We weren't in any danger."

His expression was grim. "Oh no?" Still holding the mare's reins, he slid to the ground and moved toward her.

Angrily she glared down at him. "Why can't you just

leave me alone?" she snapped. "I don't need you. Or your stupid advice."

She saw his face harden. Suddenly he dropped the mare's reins to the ground and reached up, grabbing Megan around the waist. She gasped as he lifted her easily down to the ground in front of him. She had to tilt her head back to look up at him, and that increased her anger even more. Her fists went down, fingers pulling futilely at the hands that still gripped her waist, but she could not free herself. "Let me go!" she cried wildly. "Let me go!"

"Not yet." His voice was harsh with anger. "Not till you listen to what I have to say."

"I don't need to listen to you," she spat at him. "Just leave me alone and let me do my job. Go away," she repeated. "Just go away."

He shook her then, so sharply that her teeth rattled in her head and her new Stetson fell loose to hang by its thongs down her back.

"What's wrong with you?" he growled. "Did you leave all your sense back East? This is prairie-dog country. You don't go galloping around here in half-light. One hoof in a prairie-dog hole and your mare has a broken leg. And you have a broken neck."

Megan stared at him. She heard his words. She even realized the sense of them. But they seemed to be coming from far away. His hands on her waist were burning into her flesh. Her fingers had moved from trying to pry his loose to pushing weakly against the hard muscles of his chest. Her whole body had gone crazy with his touch. Her mouth was dry, her knees weak. Under her open jacket her breasts rose and fell rapidly with the thudding of her heart.

As she raised her eyes to his, a tremor quivered over her. A tremor of desire. She pushed more strongly at his chest, conscious of the warmth coming through his shirt. She had to get away. His hard dark face was close, his eyes boring into hers. They held her fascinated.

She managed to pull her eyes away, to lower them. And they fell on his lips, full sensuous lips. She stared at them in fascination. His scent was strong in her nostrils. She felt weak, helpless. She, who had never in her life feared a man, trembled in this man's grasp, her bottom lip quivering.

With a muffled exclamation he dropped his hands from her waist, but not to release her. One moved up her back to press her body closer to his, molding it against his hard thighs, and the other cupped her chin, tilting it up, holding her face immobile.

Her hands were caught between her body and his chest; helplessly she watched his mouth as it came closer and closer. She opened her own to protest, but no words came out. And then his lips covered hers. Hard and demanding, they savaged her mouth. She tried to struggle, but it was useless. The arm that imprisoned her body was hard as iron, and the hand under her chin gripped her flesh cruelly.

His mouth devoured hers, forcing her lips open. His tongue invaded her mouth then, seeking hers. Fearfully, it retreated before his, cowering behind her teeth. But her retreat was useless. He was in control now, and he meant to stay that way. His fingers spread open on her back, molding her soft body against his hard-muscled one.

She tried to close her lips, to escape the hand that held her chin, the tongue that sought hers so insistently. But he was adamant, and though she had managed to free her hands in the struggle, they did her no good. For as hard as she beat at his back with her closed fists, her blows had no effect on him.

She knew instinctively that this was no ordinary kiss.

It had arisen out of his anger with her. It was, in its way, a kind of punishment, a further expression of his anger, not only at the events of *this* meeting, but of the ones before.

But whatever its origin, the effect of the kiss was devastating. Megan fought to keep her reeling senses under control; she could not let him do this to her.

But her blows grew softer and softer until finally her arms went up around his neck, her fingers creeping under his Stetson to entwine themselves in the dark curling hair that brushed his denim collar. Her resistance was slowly oozing out of her; she felt her knees weakening. Her body wanted to mold itself against his hardness. She no longer cared about the reason behind his kiss, only its effect on her. Her breasts were crushed against his chest; she could feel the vibrations of her thudding heart there, mingling with the beats of his.

His tongue found hers then, and a long tremulous shiver enveloped her entire body. For a second longer he held her in his embrace. Then his arms fell away and she stood there, her legs trembling, her breasts heaving as she tried to get her breath back.

He was breathing heavily, too; she saw his chest rising and falling rapidly, heard the rasp of his breath. But his voice was even as he spoke. "Let's have dinner out tonight, Megan." His mouth caressed her name, as it had caressed her lips, and she shivered again.

Megan hesitated. She wanted— But common sense asserted itself. It was bad business to have an affair with one's boss. And from what she knew of Bart Dutton, and from the quality of that kiss, that was what he had in mind. She shook her head. "No—thank you."

She did not trust herself to say anything more, but turned to the patiently waiting mare. Her legs were still trembling, but they carried her the few steps to the mare's side and she managed to swing up. Keeping the mare to a walk, she headed toward the ranch.

It was five minutes before she breathed easily again. It was that long before she dared risk a look behind her. There was no sign of Bart Dutton. The prairie had swallowed him up as completely as though he had never existed. If only he hadn't!

But she could not solve her problems that way. And she wanted to keep her job.

She settled in the saddle with a sigh. She had not bargained for this kind of a job. Or for a boss like Bart Dutton. Who would have imagined she'd run into a macho cowboy? Or that he would be able to affect her as he did? She still couldn't figure out how a man she didn't even like could do this to her. But she could not turn tail and run for Ohio. She had never been a quitter, and she didn't intend to become one now. She meant to succeed in this job, but not, she thought with a grim smile, by sleeping with the boss.

Chapter Three

❧

Megan did not see Bart for several days. When she returned to the stable, it was Pete who met her there, Pete who took her down the row of stalls, introducing her to each animal, giving her a little of their histories.

The stuffy little room she called her office was made more agreeable when two helpful cowhands pried open the other two windows. There seemed to be quite a few around, Megan thought, wondering if this was usual on a working ranch. But since they were unfailingly polite and willing to do anything she asked, she welcomed their company. The third afternoon after her arrival, however, they all seemed to have vanished again. "Where is everyone?" she asked Pete, whose regular place of business seemed to be the tack room.

"The boss told 'em—" He stopped oiling the worn saddle and swallowed. "That is, they got work to do. Can't be hanging round the stable all the time. Even when there's a pretty lass like yerself here."

Megan couldn't help smiling. "I hope I didn't get anyone in trouble."

Pete's lined face wrinkled into a grin. "Only me. The boss gave me an earful, I can tell ya. But he's gotta admit, you do your job good."

"Thank you." Megan pulled absently at the strings of her Stetson. So Bart had bawled Pete out for letting the cowhands hang around her. He was certainly keeping away from her himself, she thought as she picked up currycomb and brush. She was glad, of course; it simplified matters a lot if he kept away from her. What had happened the other morning had been some kind of fluke. She had been unstrung by their chance meeting in town and by finding that he was her boss. And, she had to admit it to herself, his blatant maleness had shaken her. She had never before met a man with so much physical appeal. It was only chemical attraction, of course. And from what she knew of the man, it was no surprise to him.

"I'm going to give Arabica a curry," she said.

"No need fer you to do that," Pete said, waving his oily rag in a vague gesture.

"I know. I enjoy it. Anyway," Megan added, "it's good for her to get used to me. She'll be dropping her foal any day now."

Pete nodded. "Sure hope everything goes right. Bart's got a special feel fer that there mare."

Megan's surprise could not quite be hidden. "I didn't think a horse would mean that much to Mr. Dutton, as an individual, I mean. I know a breeding mare is a valuable piece of property."

If Pete noticed the formal way she referred to their employer, he didn't mention it. "Bart might *look* tough," he said, "but he's got a tender place fer his horses. Arabica now, she's out of a mare that was his mama's favorite."

"His mother's—"

"Yeah." Pete's gray eyes surveyed her shrewdly. "That boy's had a hard life. Lost his mama last year."

Again Megan was forced to pause. It was hard to think of Bart Dutton as a little boy with a mother.

"Leastways he got the ranch back on its feet afore she was took. She was right proud of him."

"The ranch was in trouble?" Megan knew it was bad business gossiping about one's employer, but she couldn't help it. Maybe if she could see Bart as a person, he wouldn't be so threatening to her.

Pete nodded. "Real bad," he said. "The old man—he was a heavy drinker. Real heavy. The place was going downhill fast."

Megan was silent. For some reason she had supposed that Bart Dutton's life had been an easy one, apart from the rodeo circuit at least.

"That's why the boy hit the circuit when he was sixteen. Somehow they kept that money away from the old man. Gradually got the place back on its feet. Did better after the old man passed on. Yes, sir, that Bart, he's a boy to be proud of."

For a minute there was silence in the tack room, the only sound that of Pete's oily rag rubbing against saddle leather. Then Megan gave herself a brisk shake and moved out toward the mare's stall. As her hands moved in long soothing strokes over the mare's flanks, she considered what she had just heard.

She inhaled the warm comforting smell of the mare. She had always done her best thinking in the barn, surrounded by the smell of horses. And she had a lot of thinking to do now.

Listening to Pete had been a mistake. It was easier to think of Bart Dutton as an arrogant macho male. Knowing something of his background, thinking of him as a human being, would not help her resist his attraction. And there was no denying that she was attracted.

Even though she had not seen him since that second morning, had eaten her meals alone in the ranch house dining room, he seemed always to be on her mind. In spite of her resolutions, she had this very morning found herself at the same clump of cottonwoods where she had met Bart that first morning. Everytime she entered or left the ranch house, everytime she heard a footstep outside the office door or the sound of a horse or car in the yard, she was instantly alert, wanting to see him and knowing she shouldn't.

Absently she leaned her head against the mare's bulging side. Had coming west been a mistake? What if she couldn't free herself of this crazy feeling for Bart Dutton? What if he made another pass? Tried to kiss her again? But that wasn't likely, she told herself as she resumed currying. After all, she hadn't even seen him since that morning.

She would stick it out. At least till her month's probation was over. It wouldn't be at all ethical to leave now, not when the mare was due to deliver soon. Maybe that was why he had wanted a live-in vet, she thought, moving around to groom the mare's other side. At any rate, he needed her services—or the mare did. She couldn't even consider leaving until the foal had come.

She was currying Arabica's free-flowing mane when she heard the truck coming up the lane. Probably the cowhand Pete had sent into town for supplies, she thought, continuing with her self-imposed chore. The mare loved the attention she was getting, and her liking for Megan would serve her in good stead when the time came for her labor.

The door to the stable opened, but Megan, concentrating on her task, pretended not hear Pete say,

"Hello, boss." But when he added, obviously pleased and surprised, "Howdy, Miss Laina. I ain't seen you for a while," she couldn't help her start of surprise.

The circuit's been keeping me pretty busy," replied a warm female voice. "You know how it is."

"Yeah," Pete replied. "I'm old, but I ain't so old I've forgot what the circuit's like. Though it don't seem to be hurting you none."

Laina's laugh rang out, clear and throaty. "You're an old blarney-talker, Pete Greeves. And I like it."

Megan continued her brushing. If only they would leave the stable without seeing her. She was hot and sticky, smelling of horses, she thought wryly. And that woman with him, even though she had something to do with the rodeo, must be beautiful. She could tell it just from her voice, Megan thought. That tone of confidence didn't echo in the voices of unattractive women.

"Where's Megan?" she heard Bart ask. "I want Laina to meet her."

"She's down with Arabica," Pete said. "Spends a lot of time with that mare. You'd think it was *her* baby."

Laina's deep chuckle did nothing to relieve Megan's embarrassment. Nor did her next words. "Sounds like you got a real conscientious vet, Bart." The words sounded genuine, but they still made Megan uncomfortable. It was not clear to her exactly why, but she did not want Bart to think of her in terms of conscientiousness.

Footsteps approached the stall, and she moved around the mare so that she faced the door, her hands still moving in steady strokes. She looked up as Bart reached the stall.

"Hello, Megan. I see you've made friends with the mare." His voice was even and businesslike.

"Yes, I thought it would be useful." Megan forced

herself to meet those brilliant blue eyes. They were friendly, but that was all.

"I've brought an old friend out. To see the mare," Bart said. "And to meet you." He turned to the woman beside him, and Megan's eyes followed. What she saw confirmed her worst suspicions. This Laina was tall, nearly as tall as Bart himself. Long blond hair framed a face of classic features, and her jeans and shirt did nothing to conceal a voluptuous body.

"This is Megan Ryan, Laina. Laina Darwood. Laina and I are old friends," he said, turning back to Megan.

Again Laina gave that low attractive laugh. "Very old friends," she said, tucking her arm through Bart's. "You can't imagine the mischief we used to get into when we were kids."

Bart's laugh was deep and warm. This, Megan realized, was the first time she had heard it. "Now, Laina, no tales out of school."

"If you say so, Bart."

Suddenly conscious that she had been grooming the same part of the mare for some time, Megan moved slightly.

"The mare looks perfect," Laina said, running critical eyes over her. "She should drop you a beautiful foal."

Bart nodded. "I hope so. It's out of Thunder, you know. It'll be a while before Diablo's start coming."

Laina nodded, but her lovely face puckered into a frown. "I don't know why you insisted on buying that brute. He's dangerous, Bart."

He shrugged and laughed. "You know why I bought him. He damn near trampled out my brains that time he stomped me."

"You've been stomped before," Laina pointed out.

He shook his head, his face hardening. "That was

different. Accidents. This brute, he *meant* to do it. But he'll regret it."

Megan felt a shiver of fear run through her, and the mare moved nervously under her hands. Pity anyone who crossed Bart Dutton, she thought; the man was hard as nails.

"Speaking of the old devil, how about a ride out to the west range? We just might get a glimpse of him."

Laina laughed again. "All right, Bart. It'll be good to ride just for fun. Besides, I don't want to go soft."

"Fat chance," replied Bart. "Would you believe it, Megan, this little lady's a champion barrel racer."

"That must be exciting," said Megan, trying to keep her voice even. *Little* lady indeed! "I understand it takes a lot of skill."

Laina smiled. "Mostly it takes a good horse," she said. "The horse makes or breaks you. Maybe you'd like to try it sometime."

The offer was genuinely made. Megan had no doubt of that. Her laugh was a little strained, "I think not, Miss Darwood."

"Please call me Laina."

"All right, Laina. I'm afraid I haven't time for that sort of thing. I'm first and foremost a vet. I ride only for pleasure."

"Well, if you change your mind, I'll be glad to give you some pointers."

"That's very kind of you," Megan replied, "but I think I'll just stick to doctoring."

Laina nodded. "I can understand that. It must be wonderful to know what to do when a horse is sick." Her voice had taken on a wistful note. "It always makes me feel sad and helpless."

Somewhat to her surprise, Megan found she was liking this woman. "I know what you mean," she said. "I felt that way when I was a kid on the farm. That's when I decided to be a vet."

"It must have taken a lot of hard work," said Laina. "Years of schooling."

Megan nodded. "But it was all worth it. Just as I'm sure your winning is worth the hours of practice you do," she added generously. No matter what this woman was to Bart, Megan couldn't help feeling friendly toward her.

"I suppose so," said Laina softly. "But sometimes I wonder." And her face took on a strange faraway look.

"None of that," said Bart cheerfully, squeezing Laina's hand. "Come on, let's go have our ride."

Laina brightened. "Sure, Bart. Just a minute." She turned to Megan. "What do you think of Diablo?"

Megan's eyes flicked automatically toward Bart. "I haven't seen him. He's been out on the range since I arrived."

"Well then, you must come too," cried Laina. "The ride will be good for you. Pete, saddle Megan's horse, will you?"

Megan felt the blood rise to her face. "Oh, that's not necessary. I don't want to intru— That is, I've got work to do."

Laina turned swiftly to the man at her side. "What kind of boss are you, Bart?" she asked, laughter in her voice. "Come on now, tell Megan she's not a slave to the job."

Bart smiled, but there was no warmth in the blue eyes. "Megan knows I'm not a slavedriver. Anyway, you've jumped the gun. I was going to ask Megan myself, till you started assaulting my character."

Laina laughed."Good, then it's all settled. Pete?"

Megan hurried out of the stall, conscious of Bart's eyes on her, conscious of how small and childlike she must appear beside Laina's statuesque beauty. "That's not necessary. I'll saddle the mare myself. I'll be right with you." She caught the momentary flicker of relief in Bart's eyes and knew she had judged rightly. He didn't want Laina to think he was mistreating his new vet.

And what would she think, Megan told herself as she returned currycomb and brush to the shelf, if she knew about that morning kiss on the prairie? Again the red flooded her face and she jerked up her saddle with a sound of annoyance and hurried to Darling's stall. Fortunately Bart and Laina had gone outside and no one was there to observe her efforts to get the saddle onto the mare's back. Years of experience had taught her how to manage the difficult task in spite of her small stature. She led the mare out into the yard, where Bart and Laina were already mounted, Bart on a roan gelding and Laina on a beautiful Morgan mare.

For a moment Megan stopped, unconscious of Darling nuzzling at her shoulder. "What a horse!" she exclaimed, lost in pure admiration of the animal.

"Her name's Sunshine," said Laina, obviously pleased at Megan's response. "She's my favorite mount when I'm at home."

"Come on," urged Bart, a strange look on his face. "You two may have all day to gossip, but this is a working ranch. I've got other things to do."

Obediently Megan swung up and turned the mare after the others. Now why should Bart have such a peculiar look on his face?

But Laina only laughed at him. "Don't be a sourpuss, Bart. Besides, discussing horses hardly qualifies as gossip." She turned to Megan with a smile and a conspiratorial glance. "To get the real dirt you have to ride the circuit. Or know someone who does."

"Megan hasn't got time for that sort of thing," said

Bart, kicking his horse into a canter. "Besides, half the stuff isn't true."

Laina gave Megan a wink. "He's just afraid you'll hear what people say about him," she said, grinning, before urging the Morgan after him.

Megan, giving the eager little mare her head, did not do much wondering. It was fairly certain that gossip about Bart had to do with who was sharing his free time—and his bed. But that, Megan told herself sternly, was absolutely no concern of hers.

The horses kept to a steady canter, and finally the rhythm so seduced Megan that she forgot her worries. When she could be on a horse's back like this, nothing else seemed to matter.

After they'd ridden for some time, Bart slowed his horse to a walk and the others reined in beside him. "Over there," he said. "Look."

Megan followed the direction of his gloved hand, then drew in a quick breath of admiration. Off across the prairie the black stallion was galloping, his long stride eating up the distance, his mane streaming in the wind.

"What a sight he is!" Laina's voice was full of admiration. "No wonder you bought him, Bart." She turned to the man beside her. "He's a real beauty."

"I know."

Off to one side, unobserved, Megan watched his face. His whole expression changed as he watched, sheer joy in the horse's beauty lighting up his features. If she had needed any further confirmation this was enough. This man's love of horses ran as deep as her own.

He turned suddenly and caught her looking at him, and she wrenched her eyes away, trying to keep the telltale blush from reaching her cheeks. But she was not quick enough to miss the amusement glittering in those blue eyes. She kept her own eyes on the great stallion, glorying in his wild grace, imagining what it would be like to be astride that broad back, the prairie flying by in one big blur. God! To ride a horse like that must be the most wonderful thing in the world.

Evidently the same thought was in Laina's mind. "Oh, Bart! When you get him tamed, can I ride him?"

Bart chuckled. "Honey, nobody rides that baby but me. He's too much for any woman to handle." The glance he gave Megan then was one of clear warning.

She accepted it silently, keeping her expression calm. There was no use in arguing with a man like Bart. She just hoped she'd never have to treat the stallion. If he was wild now, he would be even wilder when Bart got through with him.

"Oh, Bart!" Laina didn't care much for this kind of male superiority either. "You know very well that handling a horse is a matter of skill, not brute strength."

Bart's lips tightened grimly. "Maybe so. But let a wild one like that take off with the bit between his teeth and you'll wish for stronger arms." He frowned. "I mean it, Laina. This stallion is off bounds. I've already laid down the law to Megan. Haven't I?"

Megan nodded. "Yes, he has." She offered Laina a small smile. "I haven't been here long, but one thing I've learned. When Bart lays down the law, it's *laid*."

Laina's chuckle was spontaneous. "She knows you pretty well, Bart."

"As long as she obeys me." Bart said, giving Megan a searching glance, "we'll get along fine."

"Of course." Laina was clearly enjoying Bart's discomfort. "Who would dream of disobeying the great Bart Dutton?" she teased.

"You would," he replied with a grin that was only slightly strained. He glanced at his watch. "Sorry, we've got to get back. This man's got work to do."

And he dug his heels into the roan and took off across the prairie.

Laina gave Megan an amused look and urged her horse after him. "He's like that," she said with a mischievous grin. "He can't take much teasing."

He wouldn't like being disobeyed, either, Megan thought with one last wistful look at the great stallion she would never get to ride.

Chapter Four

❦

It was a lovely dream. She knew somehow that it was a dream. She was out on the prairie, the sun coming over the horizon. Astride the great black stallion, she raced across the prairie, and it was just as wonderful as she had imagined it. She saw Bart then, riding up on the roan, but she touched her heels to the great black and sped away. No horse on earth could catch him. Bart couldn't stop her now.

And then came the hard hand on her shoulder. "Megan! Megan! Wake up!"

"No! No! Let me be. He won't hurt me!"

"Megan!" The hand shook her again, shook her hard, and Megan returned to consciousness abruptly. This was real. This was Bart's hand on her bare shoulder. And all she was wearing was a skimpy little gown.

"Bart! What are you doing here? Get out of my room!"

"Megan! Wake up!" His voice was hard. "I haven't time for this foolishness. I need you! It's the mare. It's Arabica's time."

"Oh!" Megan came completely awake. "I'm—I'm sorry. I'll be right out."

His nod was determined. "Don't waste any time."

"Yes, yes. I'll be right there."

He was out of the room in a second. "I'll be in the stables," he called back over his shoulder.

Megan scrambled into the clothes she had taken off, yanking on her boots and stuffing her shirt into her jeans as she ran down the hall. The mare had seemed fine that afternoon, but the foal had not turned yet. She hadn't expected her to go into labor so soon. Everything had to go right. Bart loved this mare.

Light radiated from the stables as Megan crossed the yard. She went into the tack room to pick up her bag, then hurried to Arabica's box.

The mare was down, rolling her eyes and tossing her head. Bart was beside her, speaking soothing words, stroking her neck. Megan's examination was quick and professional; her face gave her away when she turned.

"What is it?" Bart asked. "What's wrong?"

"I was afraid of this. I examined her this afternoon. The foal hasn't turned yet."

"Damn!" The curse was softly spoken; he didn't want to alarm the mare. "It'll strangle in the cord."

Megan made a quick decision. Quickly she rolled up her sleeves. "Maybe I can turn it."

His eyes were disbelieving. "You?"

"Remember me?" she asked calmly. "I'm the vet. Now, if you'll just keep her attention. Pete said this is her first."

"It is."

"That makes her more nervous."

"Do you think you can do it?" he demanded.

"I can't give you any guarantees," she said firmly. "I can only say I've done it before." She saw the question in his eyes. "Successfully." No need to tell him that it had been when she was still a child, helping her dad on the farm.

Bart said no more then, devoting his attention to the mare, and Megan turned to her task. It took all her effort to keep her nerves steady. This was not just any foal—this one was special. For Bart. And for her. She had to get this one right.

The night seemed endless, every second an hour. Megan, her hands deep within the mare, felt the sweat rolling down her forehead. Hunching a shoulder, she tried to wipe it away before it reached her eyes.

"Here," Bart's voice was gentle, and so were his hands as he loosened the bandana from around his neck and blotted her forehead. Megan swallowed over a sudden lump in her throat. For a moment she forgot the stable, the mare, the foal—everything but the man who knelt so close to her. The good male scent of him reached her, mixed with the inevitable hint of leather and horses, and she felt his nearness through her whole quivering body.

"Thank you," she whispered, her eyes caught by those so near her own.

"You're welcome, doc." His eyes were so warm she thought for a moment that he would say something more, but then he turned back to the mare.

Finally Megan turned to Pete. "I think I've got it. A rope. I need a rope."

Pete hurried off to get one, and Bart dabbed at her forehead again, his eyes full of concern. It was all for the mare, of course, but Megan drew strength from the touch of his hand.

Then Pete came hustling back with a length of rope. "Put a loop in it," Megan said.

"Easy now, girl," Bart crooned to the mare. "It won't be long. Just hold on."

Megan withdrew one hand and took the loop from

Pete. "The foal's too slippery. I'm going to get the rope around its front feet. That way we can help it out."

Pete nodded, his face set in grim lines.

Her head against the mare's sweaty flank, Megan reached far inside, seeking the foal's head. Her hands slid down, finding the front feet. It was difficult, working by feel alone where her eyes could not see, but finally she withdrew her hands and got to her feet. The remaining end of the rope she wrapped securely around her hands, and, bracing her feet, got ready. The mare moaned at the onset of another pain and Megan braced her feet and pulled.

"It's a-coming," said Pete. "I seen its hooves!"

Megan breathed deeply, waiting for the mare's next pain. "Comes another," said Pete from the mare's side, and Megan pulled again. She was concentrating on the pulling and so did not see Bart leave his place at the mare's head or send a silent glance at Pete. When his hands closed around her waist, she gasped and almost dropped the rope before she collected herself. By then the mare's contraction had eased.

For a moment Megan felt his hands burning into her flesh as they had that morning on the prairie. Then one hand slid around her ribcage until his arm encompassed her waist. It felt like a band of steel there, the softness of her breasts resting against it. Her heart thudded in her throat.

"We'll pull together," he said, his voice close to her ear, and then another contraction claimed the mare and Megan had no time for her own feelings.

She lost track of how many times they pulled. Bart's arm kept her close against his chest. He had hooked one arm around the end of the stall. She felt his hard body pressing against her back as he pulled her toward it.

She thought all the breath would be forced from her

body. The rope bit deeply into the flesh of her fingers. Then, finally, when she thought she couldn't bear it a second longer, the mare gave a convulsive snort and the foal came free with a jolt that sent them both crashing to the straw in a tangled heap.

The rope slipped from Megan's grasp, and for a moment she could only think of regaining her breath. Then, as she began to breathe more easily, she realized that as they fell Bart's hand had slipped from around her waist. His fingers were now cradling a breast. He could not be blamed, of course, since she had fallen on top of him, but with a smothered gasp she struggled to her feet and hurried to the mare's side.

Pete was there already and had the rope off the foal's legs. The mare, her ordeal over, was busy cleaning up her offspring. Being careful not to get in the way, Megan examined the foal. "A filly," she said, triumph in her voice. "She'll drop a lot of good foals for you."

Bart reached her side. "That she will. Thanks to you."

"I told you she knew her stuff," said Pete, grinning widely. "Never seen a better vet. Nor a prettier one."

Trying to grin, Megan felt almost too exhausted to move. Bart put an arm around her shoulders, "Look after them, Pete. Megan looks beat."

"And no wonder." said Pete. It's going on to dawn."

"I am kind of tired," she said. Her legs seemed to have lost all their spring. In fact, she wondered if they would move at all. Looking down at her bloody hands and arms, she managed a weak grin. "I must look a sight."

The pressure of his hand on her shoulder increased slightly. "You've even got blood on your nose," he said, a chuckle in his voice. "But Pete's right. On you anything looks good."

"Flatterer," she said, striving for a light tone.

By this time they had reached the back door. He held it for her. "Why don't you wash up in there?" He indicated the bathroom off the kitchen. "I don't know about you, but I'm too excited to sleep right away. I need a chance to calm down. How about some hot chocolate?"

Megan nodded. "Sounds good." She stood for a long moment after she shut the door behind her. All the strength seemed drained from her. Then she straightened her tired shoulders and began to unbutton her shirt. She hung it over the back of a chair and soaped her hands and arms liberally.

Catching sight of herself in the mirror, she grimaced. Her lacy bra looked incongruous when her face was smudged like this with sweat and grime. And there *was* blood on her nose. Then she shrugged. She had been a veterinarian tonight, not a woman—except for those few moments when she had been so conscious of Bart, of his hand burning on her breast.

With a sigh she began to soap her face. She couldn't afford to think about that now. She must remain a vet.

She had rinsed her face and was groping for a towel when she heard the creak of the door. Her eyes flew open with a start to find Bart standing in the doorway, a faded plaid shirt in his outstretched hand.

For a second Megan stood transfixed. Then, as she saw his eyes fall to the wisp of lace that covered her breasts, she felt the red flood her cheeks and her hand reached automatically for a towel, using it as a shield.

"Sorry." His eyes left her breasts and focused on her face. "I thought maybe you'd like a clean shirt. Yours got sort of dirty. This one's mine. I didn't like to go looking for one of yours."

"Thank you." Megan took the shirt with one hand,

keeping the towel in front of her with the other. "I'll be out in a minute."

"Good." Bart nodded. "The hot chocolate is almost ready. You look like you could use a cup."

Before she could say anything else he was gone, pulling the door shut behind him.

With fingers that trembled, Megan pulled on the shirt. There was about it that smell of sagebrush and leather that seemed so much a part of him. She flinched as she fumbled with the buttons; her fingers had begun to stiffen where the rope had bitten into them. In places welts had risen on her flesh and in other places the skin was broken.

She finished the buttons finally and turned to look in the mirror. The shirt hung on her, its sleeves reaching to past her fingertips, the bottom coming along to her knees. With her hair pulled back in its rubber fastener and the big shirt she looked almost like a little girl. A tired little girl, she thought with another sigh. Too tired even to try to tuck the shirt into her jeans.

She pushed open the door, wincing as her sore fingers twisted on the knob. Bart stood by the stove. He turned as he heard her enter the room. The smile that lit his face was one of amusement, but it did not anger her. She knew she looked funny in the too-big shirt.

The smile faded and became a look of concern. "You look exhausted. Here. Have a cup of chocolate."

"That sounds great," said Megan and without thinking she reached for the steaming cup. Her bruised fingers released it at the same time that a cry of pain broke from her lips. The cup shattered on the table, splashing hot liquid up to soak the front of her shirt.

Megan stood frozen, her mind unwilling to work. But even as she stood there, the hot material burning into her skin, Bart was by her side. He ripped the shirt from her in one violent movement. It took him only a moment longer with the bra; its flimsiness parted easily in his hands. Then she was lifted in his arms and he was crossing to the sink, depositing her on the sideboard and throwing cold water on her.

Megan squealed as the cold water hit her tender flesh, but Bart did not stop. One hand around her shoulders supported her while with the other he used a glass to liberally douse the front of her with water.

"Bart, please!" The tremor in her voice was caused not by tiredness or by the coldness of the water, but by the fact that her breasts were exposed and she knew her nipples were rising. "I'm all right. Really." She struggled to sit erect, wishing she had loosened her hair so she could shake it forward as a protective screen. "I'm not burned. But I'm awfully cold." If her shiver was not completely one of chill, he wouldn't know. "Please, give me a towel."

"You're sure?" His eyes were deadly serious. "Scalding liquids like that can give really bad burns, you know."

She nodded. "I know. But you got to me in time." She wanted to avoid his eyes, but she could not. At least while he was looking into her eyes he wasn't looking anywhere else.

Her heart rose up in her throat as she saw his eyes change, change and grow warm. She forced herself to speak. "Please, Bart. A towel. And another shirt, if you don't mind." She glanced toward the torn pieces of shirt on the floor. "I'm sorry about that."

He shrugged. "It was an old one."

She saw the red creep up under the deep bronze of his skin. "Sorry about your—"

"That's okay." Her smile was a little strained, but it *was* a smile. "It was all in the call of duty."

He nodded and turned away. "There's a towel behind you."

"Thank you." Megan reached behind her. With his back turned, she could look down at herself without embarrassment. There seemed to be no damage from the hot chocolate. She touched her flesh gingerly, but it was not tender. Bart's quick action had saved her from any real hurt. With a quick motion she pulled the rubber loop off her hair and let it loose to cover her shoulders. Then she drew the towel across her breasts.

At that moment he turned around. His shirt was unbuttoned, and he shrugged it off. "Let's try again," he said, offering it to her.

The thought of putting on his shirt, still warm from the heat of his body, made her tremble. Still, she could hardly refuse. "Okay." When she stretched out a hand for it, however, he exclaimed aloud.

"Goddamn it, girl," he cried. "No wonder you dropped the cup. Look at that hand! Let me see the other."

"I—can't." Megan's voice was low.

"Don't be stupid," he said gruffly. "I've already seen what you're trying to hide with that towel. But here, put this on."

He held the shirt for her, and Megan slid her arms into it. She felt its warmth against her skin, his warmth, and trembled. She kept her back to him after she slid down from the counter and fumbled awkwardly with the buttons. But he swung her firmly around. "Let me do that."

She knew it would take her a long time with her hands the way they were, and so she stood silent while he buttoned the shirt. She tried not to breathe, not to look at him, standing there in front of her. But she had to look somewhere. Either up into his face or into his bare chest. She didn't dare meet his eyes, not now when her heart was pounding in her throat and his fingers were so close to her flesh. But keeping her eyes on his chest was not much better. It was broad and well muscled, the chest of an athlete. And under its covering of fine dark hair she thought she could detect the beating of his heart.

As he bent closer to do the lower buttons she was enveloped in the male scent of him, and his chest brushed lightly against her cheek. She was glad then that the long sleeves hid her hands, for she had to fight not to touch him. It was only with difficulty that she did not give in to the impulse to rest her face against the broad chest so near it.

"There." He straightened and looked down at her. She was aware now of the network of thin scars that ran diagonally across his ribs into the hair and were hidden there. Pete had been right. Bart had had his share of bad spills.

The room seemed suddenly to tilt around her, and Megan swayed on her feet. Bart's hand was under her elbow instantly, and he led her to the table and settled her in a chair. Then he knelt before her. "Sit here now and let me see those hands. Both of them."

Obediently Megan stretched out her hands. First he rolled up the ridiculously long sleeves, his big fingers moving deftly. Then he examined her hands and shook his head. "Little fool. Should have worn gloves."

Megan shook her head. "Can't. Can't feel through them."

"You could have put them on after you got the rope in place."

She shrugged. "I suppose so. I didn't think."

"Neither did I," he said, his tone rueful. He rose to his feet. "Sit still. You've got to have something on those hands."

"I'll get something upstairs," she replied, making a motion to rise.

A big hand on her shoulder pushed her firmly back into the chair. "No, you won't. You'll let me do it."

Megan gave in then. She was far too tired to argue. "All right."

She slumped in the chair while she waited. What she longed for was just to put her head down on the table top and sleep. It was all she could do to keep her body erect. Her eyes seemed to keep drifting shut of their own accord.

"Megan."

Though he spoke her name softly, she jerked and her eyes flew open. "Guess I was dozing," she apologized.

He looked a little grim, but said only, "Put out your hands. This is going to sting now, so hold on."

She thought she was too tired to feel the antiseptic, but its bite was harsh. It was only by clenching her teeth that she was able to keep from crying out.

It seemed forever that he stood there, pouring antiseptic over her hands, but finally he was satisfied. He put the bottle down on the table and picked up the roll of gauze.

"Bart!" Megan stared at him as he began to wrap her hands.

"No arguing," he said firmly. "I'm the boss here." His smile took the sting out of his words. "There." He finished taping the gauze and surveyed his work with obvious satisfaction. "I should have been a doctor," he said, his grin devilish.

Megan, looking down at her gauze-swathed hands, could only giggle feebly. "Not a surgeon, I hope."

"Come here. I want to show you something." His hands slid under her armpits and lifted her to her feet. For just a moment she felt their warmth against the soft sides of her breasts. Then, with an arm around her shoulders, he led her into the living room. The great picture window overlooked the prairie. Dawn was just breaking, pearly yellow and pink against the pale blue of the sky.

They stood there, his arm companionably about her shoulders, the hot chocolate completely forgotten. "Beautiful sunrise, isn't it?" he said softly, his lips close to her ear.

"Yes," Megan whispered. "It's lovely." And it was lovely, standing close to him, his arm warm around her, the heady scent of him enveloping her. Lovely—and dangerous.

"That's what I'm calling the filly," he said. "Arabica's Sunrise."

The tears came suddenly to Megan's eyes. This was not the man she had thought she knew. This was no blustering braggart, arrogantly stepping over people, but a tender, kindhearted, feeling man.

He swung toward her, his hands on her shoulders pulling her around toward him. She saw his mouth coming, slowly, inexorably, toward her own. She could not protest, could not resist him. Her legs had lost all their strength. She was able to stay on her feet only because of the support of his arms.

His lips met hers. The kiss was gentle, tender, comforting. Megan yielded herself to it, her bandaged hands encircling his neck, her body molding itself against his hard one.

As he finished he lifted her easily into his arms. "Now I'm going to carry you to bed."

"I can walk," she protested weakly.

His own grin was smudged with fatigue. "Wanna bet? You're out on your feet."

"You don't look in exactly peak condition yourself," she said softly, for the first time noticing the dark growth of his beard.

His grin grew wider. "Listen, woman. I can carry

you with one hand!" And he swung her up in his arms and balanced her there.

Megan couldn't help squealing. "Bart! Put me down!"

He laughed, a rich full sound that she hugged to her heart. "Nothing doing. I'm carrying you up to bed. And that's that."

Fatigue was creeping up on her again; it came in waves that made her eyelids flutter shut. "You win." The words were only a mumble, but exhausted as she was she was conscious that her cheek rested against a warm bare shoulder, that if he bent his head just a little he could kiss her again.

They made the trip up the stairs without incident, Megan relaxing in the arms that held her. He pushed open the door to her room and crossed to the bed. "Sleepytime for you, brown eyes," he said as he eased his arms out from under her. Megan sighed, reluctant to lose the feel of him, wanting to stay in his arms.

"Guess I can't let you sleep in your boots," he said suddenly and proceeded to take them off, and then her socks. She felt his hands at her belt buckle, but she felt no fear. It seemed perfectly natural to have him undressing her. He tossed her jeans over a chair and lifted her so he could pull back the covers and slide her under them. "And that," he said, his voice strangely hoarse, "will have to do. I'll get my shirt in the morning. Okay?"

"Okay." Megan heard the word float out between them, but it hardly seemed to have issued from her mouth. She felt enclosed in a warm cocoon, surrounded by the scent of Bart's shirt. His warm breath caressed her forehead as he planted a kiss there. "Goodnight, sleeping beauty," he whispered.

"Goodnight, my prince." She was convinced that she was already dreaming, so it hardly mattered what she said. A smile of amusement lit his face and a look of surprise flashed briefly in his eyes before he turned away, but she had already rolled over on her side and curled up, overtaken by sleep.

Chapter Five

The sun was high when Megan woke. A glance at her watch told her it was almost nine. She should be out checking on the mare. With a smile she looked at her bandage-swathed hands. Bart would never make a doctor. She peeled the layers away. Her fingers were sore, but they were already beginning to heal. With a little care she could get along fine.

She threw back the covers and smiled again. She liked wearing his shirt; it was almost as though she had a part of him still with her. Vaguely she remembered him carrying her up here, putting her to bed. It seemed to her that they had spoken to each other, but it was all covered by a fine haze of fatigue, like a picture seen through a frosted window—indistinct and hazy.

She was soon dressed, and then, breakfast forgotten, she hurried toward the stables, eager to see the new filly and the mare.

She found Pete straddling a chair outside the tackroom door. "Morning, doc. Sleep well?"

"Like a log." Megan laughed. "I never heard a thing.

Where's Bart?" she asked, unable to keep the eagerness out of her voice.

Pete's knife didn't miss a stroke as he carved at a piece of wood. "He left 'bout eight. Rode over to the Darwood place. Said he'd be back after lunch."

Megan tried to keep the smile on her face. "How's the mare?"

"Doing fine," Pete said. "The filly, too."

"I'll just go over and take a look," she said.

"Fine. I'm jest gonna sit here and soak up some more sunshine."

Megan forced herself to hold her head high as she walked on into the stable. So Bart had gone over to see Laina. He wanted to tell her about the new colt, no doubt. Sudden tears flooded Megan's eyes so that she had to slow her steps once she was inside the stable's coolness. Of course he'd gone to see Laina. What had happened last night didn't really mean anything. It had been a special occasion. They were both high after the foal's birth, exhausted and yet strung up. And there had been that sexual tension between them from the very first. She supposed it was only natural for something to happen when fatigue lowered the barricrs.

The kiss had been nothing special; just a friendly token of celebration. She could not keep the blood from her cheeks at the recollection of last evening's events. First he had seen her without her shirt, the wisp of bra the only covering for her breasts. Then, when she spilled the chocolate, he had ripped off the shirt and seen her breasts bare. And when he put her to bed, he had taken off her jeans. He had seen practically everything there was to see.

But it hadn't meant anything, she told herself again. She had been foolish to think that it did. She blinked rapidly, trying to keep back the tears as she leaned over the railing to look into the box stall. The mare looked completely recovered, and the foal, its spindly legs looking hardly strong enough to hold it, was nursing greedily.

Megan smiled. Everything looked fine here. The mare raised her head from the hay and licked the foal's fuzzy back. The tears spilled over then, and Megan stifled a sob. Baby animals always made her feel sentimental, but there was more to this than that. At the moment the mare had shown her mother love, Megan had experienced an almost physical pain. She wanted a child. She wanted it so bad it hurt. But that was not the worst of it. In her mind she saw the child—a black-haired, blue-eyed baby. Bart Dutton's baby!

She wiped her eyes with the back of her hand and moved into the stall to examine the pair. Everything seemed to be in order. By the time she had finished looking them over, she had herself in hand again. This kind of behavior was stupid and not at all called-for. Just because they had shared in the birth of the foal, just because he had treated her with tenderness and concern—certainly that didn't mean anything special to him. He was used to dealing with women. He knew how to treat them, whether it was by punishing them with kisses or tenderly tucking them in after a hard night's work.

Megan rubbed the mare's velvet nose absently. Here was a problem she hadn't considered. Before taking this job she had recognized that she might not like the climate, or the working conditions, or the boss even. But she had never once thought that she might fall in love with him! And now that seemed to have happened. What else could imagining herself with Bart's child mean?

Frowning, she gave the colt a swift pat and left the stall, closing the door carefully behind her. This kind of thinking would get her nowhere. Clearly she couldn't walk off the job without a reason. And what reason could she give? She had nothing to complain about, nothing except his rather high-handed treatment of her. And to use that as an excuse would only make her look ridiculous.

Straightening her shoulders, Megan returned to the sunshine and Pete. She had never been one to run away from her problems. She would just have to work her way through this one.

"They both look fine," she said, dropping down on a convenient rock. "I'm so glad everything worked out."

"You and me both," said Pete. "You should've heard the boss this morning. He was raving over the great job you did. Just about wore out his tongue carrying on about it."

Megan managed a smile.

"Didn't do me no harm neither," said Pete. "Me having been responsible for yer hiring, so to speak." He cast her a sly look.

"I'm glad I helped you get in good with the boss," she replied. "But I have a suspicion you really didn't need my help. You've been with Bart for a long time, haven't you?"

"Yep." Pete frowned thoughtfully. "Was here when the boy was born. Watched him grow up." His eyes took on a faraway look. "Spunky little feller. Apple of his mother's eye."

Megan heard the feeling in the old man's voice, but did not interrupt.

"Taught him how to ride, I did. And rope. His daddy being already overly fond of the bottle. Yeah, never had no family of my own. But that boy . . ."

Megan sighed softly. "How lucky he was to have you."

Pete's smile was tender. "Luck was on both our

sides, I reckon." His smile faded. "I been real proud of
the boy. But I'm getting worried lately."

Megan's heart jumped. "Why?"

"That boy needs a woman."

Megan's tone was more revealing than she knew. "I
don't suppose he needs to worry about women. They're
probably climbing all over him."

Pete gave her a sharp look and snorted. "I didn't say
women. Any man can find him that. I mean *one*
woman. To settle down with. Raise himself a family."
He shook his head. "He's turning thirty this year. Been
on the rodeo circuit too long. Busted a lot of bones,
too. Time he retired."

There was silence as Megan struggled not to ask the
question foremost in her mind. Finally she gave in. "I
thought Laina . . ."

Pete shrugged. "So did lotsa people, but it ain't happened yet. Bart seems willing enough. Maybe she ain't
ready to retire yet. The circuit can get in yer blood.
And barrel racing don't break no bones."

Megan asked no further questions. She could not
imagine herself postponing being Bart's wife. Not if the
chance was offered her. But of course it would not be.

Suddenly she found Pete's company oppressive. She
needed to be alone. "Guess I'll take a ride."

Pete did not look up from his whittling. "Darling's in
the back corral. Best stay away from the west range,
though. Even last night won't save yer skin if Bart
catches you messing round that stallion."

"Okay." She kept her voice even. Until that very
moment she had not thought of Diablo, but now that
Pete had brought him to mind, she was determined to
go to the west range. Bart might know rodeo horses,
but his stupid rules about the stallion could well interfere with her efforts to treat him if he should become ill
or hurt. Besides the fact that she was eager to put

into effect certain techniques she had learned for gaining the confidence of difficult animals, she badly needed something to take her mind off Bart Dutton and his visit to Laina. The Darwood ranch lay east of the Rocking D. With any luck at all Bart would never know she had been near the stallion.

As always, the pleasure of riding helped to ease her tension. Her gloves protecting her still tender hands, she kept the mare to a fast walk, mindful of the ever-present danger of prairie-dog holes.

The sun was warm on her head, and she reached over her shoulder and pulled her Stetson up to put it on. She let her eyes drift out over the prairie. The sagebrush was high, already drying in the summer sun. The tumbleweed rolled gently in the slight breeze. In spite of her unlooked-for feelings for Bart, life here was good. She was surrounded by horses and beautiful country. She could hardly ask for a better situation.

She reached the watering hole with its sparse clump of cottonwoods and let the little mare drink before she slipped down and tied her. Searching out a cool spot, she stretched out in the shade, willing herself to relax. She still felt tired from the night before, but it *had* been a good night's work, a night to be proud of, she thought with a smile as she tilted her Stetson over her eyes.

Though her eyes were closed and her limbs relaxed, her senses were alert. Riding up to the place, she had spied the stallion off in the distance, a small herd of mares at his heels. She had not seen him gallop off, shooing them to safety, so she was that far ahead at least. The gaining of an animal's trust was never an easy thing, but the stallion's past had predisposed him to mistrust and fear men. It would take time, maybe a great deal of it, to overcome this initial wariness, but she knew it could be done.

Diablo did not come close enough to water, but an hour later when she eased herself erect, she saw that he had edged somewhat nearer. Enough for one day, she told herself with satisfaction, as she moved slowly to untie the mare and swing up.

It was shortly after lunchtime and her stomach was grumbling emptily when she made her way to the kitchen. Mrs. Grean, her spotless white apron covering an ample stomach, attempted an unsuccessful frown. "No breakfast *and* no lunch," she said. "Tsk! Tsk! You'll be melting away to nothing, child."

"I'm sorry to bother you between meals," Megan said.

"As if I'm not used to it," the housekeeper said with a smile. "The boss never eats on time anyway.

"Now!" She gestured to a chair. "You just sit yourself down there and I'll bring you a nice roast-beef sandwich and a glass of milk."

Megan couldn't help laughing. "Milk? Mrs. Grean!"

The housekeeper chuckled. "A bit of calcium never hurt a body. And after the work you did last night, you need some good food."

"I'm willing, Mrs. Grean," Megan said with a smile. "My stomach is really empty."

It took the housekeeper only minutes to return with a hearty roast-beef sandwich on home-baked bread. Megan eyed it hungrily before she bit into it. "Thank you—it looks delicious."

She was finishing the last crust and considering having another when the door opened to admit Bart.

"Mrs. Grean, where—" He stopped as he saw Megan and tossed his Stetson onto its hook. "There you are. Just the person I want to see." He crossed the room in three quick strides. "How are your hands this morning?" he asked.

"Much better," she replied, offering them for his inspection.

He nodded. "Yes, they'll do. And how's the rest of you?"

"Fine," she said, willing herself not to blush under the scrutiny of his eyes. She was determined to treat last night as nothing special. She certainly didn't want him to think she believed anything else. "I've been out looking at the new filly."

"Arabica's Sunrise," he said, his eyes meeting hers in a moment of warmth. "You should see her, Mrs. Grean, the prettiest little filly in the country."

The housekeeper put a cup of steaming coffee in front of him. "As if you hadn't told me that very thing already ten times over." She smiled at Megan. "Such a man for his horses, he is."

Bart laughed. "That won't get you much sympathy," he said. "Not from a confirmed horse lover like Megan."

Mrs. Grean joined in their laughter. "Aye, I'd more or less guessed that." And she bustled off with the dirty dishes.

Bart turned back to Megan, who was finishing her milk. "So you're feeling all right?"

"Yes," she said, wishing he wouldn't look at her quite so closely. It was one thing to remind herself objectively that last night meant nothing and quite another to keep her body from responding to the closeness of his.

Bart gulped down the rest of his coffee. "Great," he said, pushing back his chair. "Hustle upstairs now and put together some things. We're flying down to Billings to look at a new mare. I want your opinion on her. Can you be packed in an hour?"

It took Megan a second to gather her wits. "I—I guess so."

"Good. Oh, we'll be staying overnight. See you in an hour." And he was gone before she had a chance to think of any questions, let alone ask them.

She carried her empty glass to the sink.

"Thank you, dear. You're an orderly, neat person," said the housekeeper. Her eyes twinkled. "If I were you, I'd be picking a pretty dress to take along. I heard him make reservations at a fancy restaurant."

"Mrs. Grean!" Megan's heart seemed to leap up in her throat.

"Well, if he don't want a person to hear such things, he shouldn't be making the calls right here in my kitchen," and she gave Megan a big wink as she plunged her hands back into the sink full of soapy water.

Megan hurried toward the staircase. Dinner at a fancy restaurant! She had nothing suitable for that. The few dresses she had brought with her were the serviceable kind, for churchgoing and the like. And shoes! She took the stairs to the second floor two at a time, her tiredness forgotten as she concentrated on woman's age-old problem—what to wear.

Chapter Six

At first Megan found the plane trip exciting. She had never been up in a small plane before, and after the first moments of fear as the ground fell away, it was fascinating to look down at the countryside. But eventually her eyelids began to sink and Bart grinned at her. "Lean back and sleep a little. I don't want you to conk out on me tonight. We've got things to discuss."

Megan wanted to ask him what kinds of things. He was piloting the two-seater himself and there was no one else to hear, but the look in his eyes indicated that he meant what he said. And she *was* tired. As she made herself comfortable she wondered briefly how he could look so bright and wide-awake after the night they had had.

Her eyes were shut, but Megan could see his face clearly. The strong nose, the jutting chin, the flashing blue eyes that seemed to hold so much invitation. His skin was bronzed dark by the sun, the scar on his forehead a thin white line. She would have to ask him how he got that one, she thought as she drifted off to sleep with a contented sigh.

A rented car waited for them at the little airfield outside of Billings. It took them directly to a downtown motel. Bart left her there in a pleasantly decorated room. "Got some stuff to take care of," he said. "Why don't you rest some more? I'll pick you up at seven-thirty for dinner." His eyes were warm. "I trust Mrs. Grean told you to bring something nice to wear."

Megan colored. "How—how did you know?"

His teeth flashed white in the bronzed face. "Trade secret," he said. "Don't worry about it. Just get yourself togged out in your glad rags and be ready to hit the town."

Megan nodded, her eyes bright with anticipation. "I'll be ready."

He was gone down the hall, his long legs carrying him swiftly away. Megan turned back into the room and shut the door. She did not feel at all tired now. Lying down was the last thing she wanted to do.

On an impulse she lifted the phone. "Are there any dress shops nearby?" she asked the clerk.

Half an hour later, face washed and hair freshly combed, she ventured out, stopping first at the desk to get the directions that had been promised her.

It had been years since she'd been so excited about buying a dress. She felt almost like a teenager getting ready for her first date, she told herself as she entered the first boutique on her list.

Six dresses later Megan stood before the dressing-room mirror and smiled. This was the dress she'd been looking for. It was rather expensive, but she hadn't had a new dress for so long, and it was just perfect. It was of pale-peach silk, its draped bodice emphasized the swell of her breasts and its wide cumberbund showed off her slender waist before the skirt flowed out in becoming fullness over femininely rounded hips.

The salesgirl appeared in the doorway. "Oh!" Her admiration was clearly genuine. Megan was sure of that.

"It's perfect," Megan said. She looked down at her serviceable brown pumps. "I need some shoes."

The salesgirl smiled. "I know just the pair. Two doors down. Cream-colored sandals. Just a few straps and heels." Her glance was wistful. "What I wouldn't give for hair like that!"

Megan smiled her thanks and hurried off to finish her purchases.

She was ready five minutes early. She looked perfect with her new dress, her new shoes, her hair piled in a Grecian kind of knot that made her look taller and exposed the lines of her slender neck. Around her throat she wore a small pendant, the polished brown stone lying in the gentle curve between her breasts. Now the vee made by the crossed drape of her bodice seemed terribly deep, and she eyed it anxiously.

She had only wanted to dress up, to look nice and recapture some of the fun of those youthful years that she had missed in her determined quest for her degree. But the woman who stared back at her from the mirror looked far more sophisticated than Megan felt. The only apparent sign of her apprehension was the rosy cast of her cheeks and a shine in the velvet brown eyes. Well, she told herself defiantly, she was merely obeying orders. He had told her to dress up and she had.

A brisk knock on the door caused her to jump slightly, and she composed her features carefully before crossing to open it.

For a moment she was too stunned by the sight of the man standing there to consider what he was thinking of her. In a wheat-colored suit with a cream-colored shirt and pale-orange tie and wearing a wheat

Stetson and light boots, he looked as if he'd just stepped out of an ad. The light colors set off the bronze of his skin, and his hair seemed even blacker against the pale hat.

Bart spoke first. "Wow!" The word emerged with quiet emphasis. "What a dress!" He grinned at her. "If you brought that from Ohio, the Rocking D must have been quite a shock to you."

"Oh no, I didn't." She felt suddenly embarrassed. "I didn't have anything—appropriate. And I wasn't tired anymore. So—I went shopping."

His eyes moved over her familiarly, causing warmth to flood her body. "You look great." His smile broadened. "Hungry?"

"Starving," Megan replied, realizing for the first time how long ago it seemed since her roast-beef sandwich.

"Good." He pulled the door shut behind her and slipped the key into his pocket, then tucked her arm through his. "I'm off to show you one of Billings's best restaurants."

For Megan the evening began to take on the quality of a dream. From the moment they entered the restaurant they were greeted with deference. Everyone seemed to know Bart, yet no one intruded on their privacy. As the waiter shook out her napkin for her and placed it carefully in her lap, Megan flushed again. This kind of living was far outside her means.

"You look lovely," Bart whispered as the waiter moved off to get their cream of cauliflower soup. "Everyone's wondering where I found you." He chuckled. "I daresay you'll do a lot for the cause of women veterinarians tonight."

Megan accepted the compliment with a half-smile. "Good looks don't necessarily eliminate brains," she said. "And as I remember it, you weren't too sold on the idea of a woman vet."

His smile was warm. "That was before I saw you in action. After last night I'm fully convinced."

The soup arrived then, followed by the salads, then the steaks, butterflied and grilled to tender perfection, served with baked potatoes smothered in sour cream and hot crispy rolls. Megan groaned when she saw her plate. "I'll never be able to finish it."

Bart chuckled. "Nonsense. You've hardly eaten a thing today. A growing girl . . ." His chuckles deepened into laughter at her frown. "A hardworking woman like you needs to eat."

"You sound just like Mrs. Grean," said Megan with an impish smile.

"Ah, but I don't look like her," Bart replied. "Fortunately for you, since the two of you would look a fine sight out there on the dance floor!"

The bantering had helped to ease Megan's tensions, but the thought of being in his arms recalled to her quite vividly that morning kiss on the prairie and the one of last night. She should not be thinking such things, she told herself sternly. Bart just meant for them to spend an enjoyable evening together. It would go no further than that.

For the first time since that afternoon she thought of the horse they had come to inspect. "Is this a breeding mare we're going to see tomorrow?" she asked. "You'll not find another as beautiful as Arabica easily."

Bart nodded. "That's business. Tomorrow's for business. Tonight's for fun. Okay?"

"Okay," Megan replied, her heart jumping up into her throat. It was unfair for a man to be as blatantly male as the one who sat across the table from her, his blue eyes warm and admiring. "Tell me about yourself," he said. "Why did you decide to be a vet?"

Megan chewed thoughtfully on a bite of steak as she considered this. "I grew up on a farm. In Ohio. It wasn't very big." She smiled, her face aglow at the memory. "But we had a couple of cows, a couple of horses, assorted dogs, cats, and chickens. There was always some animal getting hurt or having babies. And I seemed to have a knack for caring for them." The smile faded from her face as the memories came flooding back. "Sometimes, though, there was nothing I could do." She swallowed over the sudden lump in her throat. "That hurt." She blinked rapidly against the onslaught of tears. "So I decided to do something about it. To go to school and learn what to do. And I did."

"So your folks sent you to school."

She hesitated a moment too long before saying yes.

"You worked your way through vet school," he said, shaking his head.

She knew there was no use denying it. "My folks couldn't help. They could barely make ends meet. But they gave me all kinds of emotional support."

"Why didn't you go back to the farm?" he asked.

She had to blink again. "It was gone by then. They were both killed in an accident, in my senior year. I had to sell the farm. There were debts."

"Of course. That's why you were free to come west."

She nodded. His quiet, noncommittal tone helped her regain her calm when sympathy would have released the tears that lay so near.

"What about you?" said Megan. "What made you go into the rodeo?"

It was as if a shutter had slipped down over his eyes, hiding his innermost self from her, yet his voice did not change. "The excitement, I guess. Boy wanting to prove himself a man."

She did not believe this, though she might have without Pete's revealing comments. She did not mention that, however, merely asking, "And is it exciting?"

He shrugged. "If you call broken bones exciting. The thrill wears off after a while."

"Then why do you still do it?" Megan asked. "Surely you've proved yourself a man by now." Now, she thought, now he would tell her he was waiting for Laina to quit.

He grinned. "Habit, I guess. A person gets used to a certain way of life. And the pay's not bad. If you stay on top." Absently his fingers traced the thin scar on his forehead.

"Where did you get that one?" she asked.

"This?" His fingers stopped abruptly. "Diablo gave it to me—the day he just missed stomping my brains out."

Megan shivered. "Why didn't you quit then?"

His face hardened. "You may be an expert on horses," he said, "but when it comes to men . . . I couldn't have people saying I'd turned yellow."

Megan's tone was serious. "I can't imagine anyone thinking that of you, let alone saying it."

His eyes grew warm again. "Thanks. But rodeo riders are a hard lot. We have to be. And we don't give the other fellow much room for doubt."

"But surely you could quit now," she said.

"I suppose so." He sipped his coffee slowly and reflectively, his eyes sober over the rim of his cup. "I've been giving it some serious thought this year. It might be nice to stay home and run the ranch for a change."

Megan clenched her suddenly tense hands in her lap. Now, now he would mention Laina, would tell her that it was because of Laina that he had delayed leaving the circuit.

But he returned the cup to its saucer and lifted a dark eyebrow. "Do you want some dessert?"

Megan shook her head. "No thanks. The meal was

delicious." For some odd reason she felt a sense of relief. If he did not tell her about Laina, perhaps they were only friends. At least, she could hope so.

"Would you like to dance?" Bart asked.

Megan knew she should say no. To be in his arms was far too dangerous. But she knew she could not refuse. For this one night, at least, she could pretend that the man she loved loved her, that they were spending a wonderful evening together. "Yes, Bart," she replied softly. "I would like that."

As in a dream, she got to her feet and moved onto the small dance floor. His hand moved smoothly around her waist as she stepped into his arms. She felt the warmth of it through the silk of her dress. Even with her high heels, the top of her head just reached his chin, her cheek rested against his jacket front. She felt the heat of his body through shirt and jacket, as his scent enveloped her. To her surprise, that scent still suggested leather and horses. She sighed, trying to control the chaos of feelings that threatened to overwhelm her.

How vividly her memory presented her with a picture of his chest—darkened by exposure to the sun, yet not as dark as his face, the fine mat of dark hair spreading across the upper part before narrowing to disappear beneath his belt. And the network of scars, their thin slashes contrasting sharply with the darkness of his skin.

She experienced a fierce surge of tenderness. She wanted to cradle this man against her, to take his scarred body in her arms and offer him comfort. She was being ridiculous, she told herself. Bart Dutton didn't need her—not for comfort or for anything else. Yet the feeling would not be vanquished. It hovered in the back of her mind even as she fell more and more under the spell of this man.

His arm gathered her closer, and she felt her breasts flatten against his chest, and, remembering how he had seen her only the night before, she felt her breasts tingling. There was no use denying the fact. She wanted this man; she wanted him as she had never wanted a man before. His every touch stirred her senses into a heightened awareness of him.

They danced silently, his chin against the top of her head, his arm drawing her closer and closer until she could feel his hard thighs through the thin material of her dress, and rational thought deserted her. She was no longer capable of considering tomorrow, of remembering that it was poor business policy to have an affair with one's boss. The only thing that mattered was Bart's arms around her, Bart's body against her own.

He seemed to sense that, for when they finally left the dance floor, he kept her close against his side as he paid the bill, then drove the short distance back to the motel. His arm remained around her waist as they made their way down the hall to her room. And when he took the key from his pocket and unlocked the door, it seemed perfectly natural for him to draw her inside and shut the door after them.

He stared down at her for one suspense-filled moment, and then he pulled her into his arms and covered her lips with his. It was a long kiss. His lips explored hers, searching, seeking, uncovering nerve endings that she had not known she possessed. Her lips opened under his, willing, even anxious, for his exploration, and her body pressed eagerly against his, fitting itself against his hardness. His hands slid down from her waist, molding her roundness, drawing her unprotesting body even closer against him so that she could feel the hard proof of his desire pressing into her.

The kiss left her breathless, clinging to him for support. His hands moved to the top of her dress, slipping it down over her smoothly rounded shoulders, his lips moving swiftly over the exposed flesh.

"Oh, Megan!" he groaned. "You're beautiful, so beautiful." His hands had found the zipper to her dress and pulled it smoothly down so that the dress slid over the roundess of her hips to fall in a heap at her feet. He drew in a breath as he gazed at her. "Just as beautiful as I remember," he breathed, his voice hoarse with desire.

Gently he ran the tip of one brown finger around the top of her bra where the white flesh mounded above the wispy lace. Then his hands slid downward, cupping her breasts, his palms against her nipples. A moan came from Megan's slightly open lips, she felt her nipples straining against the material as if they yearned for the touch of his hand.

"So beautiful," he whispered, his hands sliding around her to unhook the bra, letting it fall to the floor with her dress.

"Ohhhh!" Megan could not help herself as his fingers explored her back, moved slowly around to enclose her bare breasts. Between his seeking fingers her nipples grew even more erect, and deep within her she felt the rising of desire. He was flame, fire. And she was molten, his to mold as he pleased.

His hands left her breasts to tear at his jacket, his tie, his shirt. To her surprise she saw her own hands helping. Then his chest was bare, and without waiting for his reaching hands she threw herself against him, one long shuddering moan of pleasure issuing from her lips as her breasts crushed against his flesh.

"Oh, Megan, Megan," he groaned, pulling her even closer. "I want you so much."

As if she were a child, he lifted her in his arms and

carried her to the bed. At the bedside he stood her on her feet and knelt before her, his deft hands slipping off the sandals, then moving slowly up her pantyhose-clad legs. Up, up, under the silk of her half slip, until they fastened on the elastic around her waist and with one smooth movement stripped slip, pantyhose, and panties from her.

She heard another indrawn breath as he knelt there before her, and then his mouth began to leave a trail of kisses up her inner thigh until they reached the center of her ecstasy.

The feelings that swept her were so strong she thought her knees would buckle. His mouth continued, moving up over the smooth whiteness of her belly, up, up, to the breasts that yearned to feel its touch. He lingered there for a moment before moving up to again enfold her mouth and topple her gently backward on the bed.

He stood looking down at her for a moment, and her need for him was so great that without thinking she raised her arms to him. "Just a minute, sweetheart. Let me get out of these." He pulled off his boots, dropped trousers and shorts, and stood before her.

Megan's heart pounded under her exposed breast. How hard and lean his body was. Her eyes traced the dark chest hair down, down, to where his desire was so clearly in evidence.

"Now," he said and lowered himself upon her. She felt the hairy roughness of his legs against hers, the maleness of him seeking entry, and she opened herself to him, fully and freely. There was no thought in her of the future. There was no future beyond this moment.

But though he was ready, he did not take her yet, using mouth and hands to drive her further into desire.

"Oh, please!" she begged, knowing nothing but this terrible, all-consuming desire for him.

"Say you want me, sweetheart." He looked down at her, eyes glazed with passion. "Say you want me as much as I want you."

He took one nipple between his teeth, gently teasing it, and she writhed against him, wrapping her arms around his neck, trying to pull him back down against her.

"Oh, God," he groaned. "I can't wait any longer, sweetheart. I have to have you now." And he matched his actions to his words, entering her carefully.

Megan gasped and pulled him to her. "Oh yes, Bart! Now! Please!"

His breath came in great gasps against her throat as he drove into her, and her body arched to meet his with glad expectancy, savoring the feel of it, hard and muscular against her own. Her fingers dug into his shoulders as her desire mounted higher. She was lost now, lost in a chaos of feeling that wrenched every cell in her body, wrenched it into an agony of ecstasy that was beyond imagining. She cried out at the final moment and heard his answering exclamation. Then they were drifting down, slowly, gently, in a cloud of peaceful comfort.

When he rolled off, his arms did not release her, but pulled her close against his side, her head fitting naturally into the hollow of his shoulder. She lay there in utter relaxation, not moving, not thinking, conscious of nothing but great contentment.

The shrill ringing of the phone caused them both to jump. Megan's hand went out automatically. "Hello." Her voice changed suddenly. "Pete! What is it?"

Beside her she felt Bart stiffen. He took the phone from her fingers, and, suddenly cold, she clutched at the sheet.

Bart's voice was clipped and businesslike. "What is it, Pete? . . . Are you sure?"

Megan longed to reach out and touch him, to find her way back to the dream that the shrilling of the phone had so rudely shattered, but she felt paralyzed. This was not the tender lover she had just known. This was the cowboy she had run into in Miles City. And it was insane for her to be in bed with him now, just as insane as it would have been the first day she met him.

Bart hung up the phone just as she glanced at her watch. Two a.m. The realization hit her all at once. It was two a.m. and Pete knew that Bart was in her room. She felt the shame flooding over her. Pete, who had been her friend. What would he think?

"Megan." Bart's hand was heavy on her arm. "We've got to go. Pete says the mare's down. He can't find anything wrong. But she won't get up."

Megan nodded, clutching the sheet around her. "I'll get dressed right away."

"Good girl."

She swallowed her retort. She was not a girl. She was a woman. That much he should know for sure. But she hurried into her clothes and allowed him to hustle her out to the car.

It wasn't until they reached the plane that she began to think rationally again. "We didn't get to see the mare. You'll have to call in the morning."

Bart's hand left the wheel long enough to pat her knee. "Don't worry yourself about it. No sweat. I didn't have an appointment yet."

Megan felt a cold hand of apprehension clutch her heart. "You didn't have—"

"I meant to make it tomorrow," he said cheerfully.

"But you told me—" She forced the words out with a stiff tongue.

"I know." His expression didn't change.

"You made the restaurant reservation."

"Of course." He laughed. "I can look at Jim Carvel's stock anytime, but I couldn't take you to that restaurant without a reservation. I thought you deserved a reward for your job on the mare. Me, too."

His eyes flickered over the instrument panel. "Better try to get some sleep. I'll need you alert when we get home."

A sharp retort sprang to Megan's lips, but she bit it back. There was no use talking to him. Obviously she had been carried away by her own feelings. It was hardly Bart's fault that what she had hoped was the beginning of an intimate relationship had been for him just a little fling. His intentions were good in his own eyes. He had only meant to make her feel good, and he was within his rights in supposing that a night with the big man would do that.

It was her own fault, she thought with irritation as she tried to relax in the seat. Hadn't she known the first second she saw him that the man meant trouble? Hadn't she known that he belonged to Laina? Known it and tried to ignore it?

Well, she did not mean to do that again. In the future she would remember. Remember her place, she told herself bitterly.

The trouble with the mare turned out to be a simple thing, and Megan soon had her on her feet. Aching with weariness, she allowed Bart to accompany her to her bedroom door, where he dropped a kiss on her forehead. "Sorry our trip got messed up," he said, his face showing his own fatigue. "I'll make it up to you."

"There's no need," she said quietly, and to her relief he did not pursue the matter.

"Sleep late in the morning. We'll call you if you're needed," he said, and she nodded.

In a matter of moments she was stripping off her clothes and crawling between the sheets, not even bothering to look for a gown. Exhausted in mind and body, she sank immediately into a deep sleep.

Chapter Seven

Megan woke late the next morning. Though her body had not a mark on it, she felt bruised from head to toe, emotionally and physically. She would have to reconsider staying on here, she thought, but for the present she pushed the thought aside. Bart would be gone on the circuit soon. She would just avoid him until then. When he was gone, there would be time enough to think.

She dressed slowly, then made her way down the stairs. It was late; Bart should be about his business now. She could go get her breakfast in peace.

He did not appear to be in the stable yard as she went out, and she let out a sigh, whether of relief or disappointment she wasn't sure. She spent some time with the mare and foal, fighting the sadness that threatened to overwhelm her when she saw them together. The foal should be a cause for happiness, she told herself. Something to be proud of. After all, that it was alive and well was largely due to her efforts. That should make anyone feel good.

Finally she saddled Darling and rode out into the prairie, seeking the peace that it had so often brought her. Without thinking she pointed the mare west. Just to get a glimpse of the stallion would be enough. There was comfort in his wild grace.

But she did not stay long on the west range. Not knowing where Bart was, she did not like to risk meeting him there. And besides, she would have to face up to the truth, sooner or later. She was in love with Bart Dutton. That was very clear to her. The problem was that she didn't know what to do about it.

She supposed the sensible thing would be to leave. But where was she to go? She had spent most of her remaining savings getting here. It would take time to get a new job. Time and references. She had not been here long enough to get even a month's wages, and all her references would have to come from back East. No, she would have to stay on, for a while at least. But she was determined about one thing. There was not going to be any repetition of last night. The memories of that night would haunt her for the rest of her life; she did not intend to add to them. No matter how much she might long for the feel of his body against her own.

She moved restlessly in the saddle, and the mare shifted skittishly beneath her. "It's all right, old girl." Megan patted the mare's glossy neck. "I'm just a silly romantic."

As they approached the stables Megan was dismayed to see Laina's Morgan mare standing patiently at the hitching post. But she had already been seen. Laina came out of the stable, the sun glinting in her golden hair, to wave an arm and holler. Megan had no choice but to dismount and join her.

"Hi." Laina's greeting was genuinely friendly.

"Hi." Megan tried to make her voice cheerful. "I've been for a ride. I love the prairie."

Laina nodded. "I know. I just came over to tell you goodbye. I'm taking to the circuit again. Maybe when I get back we can have lunch together. I'd like for us to be friends."

Megan forced herself to smile. "That would be nice," she replied. If this woman were not Bart's future wife, she would have welcomed her as a friend. Now, with her love for Bart throbbing within her, friendship with Laina could only bring more pain into her life. But of course she could not let on to any of this.

"I'm glad I didn't miss you," Laina said, extending a strong hand. "I thought we might have to leave before you returned. And I didn't want to do that."

"I hope you're having a successful season," Megan said.

Laina smiled and shrugged her magnificent shoulders. "My horse is in great shape. Me, too. I don't think this little layoff has hurt us."

Bart's chuckle raised the fine hairs on the back of Megan's neck. She turned to face him as he grinned at Laina. "You're always in great shape."

Laina smiled. "I do my best."

"You do indeed." Bart left the shade of the stable and came toward them. "I'll be over with the trailer in about an hour. Okay?"

"Okay." Laina sprang into the saddle with a grace that would have done any cowboy justice. "See you when I get back."

Megan, watching her ride away, kept a determined smile on her face. She had no intention of letting Bart know how much the previous evening had meant to her.

"Where were you riding?" he asked softly, and she moved automatically to put more distance between them.

"No place in particular," she replied.

"You should be resting," he said. "After two nights like we've had, you must be exhausted."

"I'm all right," she replied. "I'm stronger than I look."

The glance he gave her was one of speculation. It made her skin feel peculiar and her body respond in a way that frightened her. "Were you looking at Arabica and the foal?" she asked, hoping to distract him.

"Yes." He was right beside her as she moved back inside, and she realized that she had made a mistake. She should have stayed outside with him. Here she was alone. Alone and vulnerable, she thought, her palms going clammy. It was one thing to decide, out there on the prairie, that her love for Bart was not going to get her anywhere, that she was not going to let him use her, but here, close to him, here with the clean Western scent of him heady in her nostrils, she could not deny her body's response to his. If he kissed her, if he touched her, would she have the strength to tell him no?

His arm slid around her waist, and her body ignited at the touch, even as her mind screamed warnings. But she hadn't the strength to move away.

"Beautiful little filly, isn't she?" Bart said.

Megan nodded, for the moment not trusting herself to speak. Just hold on, she told herself. He would be gone soon, in less than an hour. Then she would be able to get herself in line.

His arm gathered her close against his side. She felt the heat of his body against hers and longed to turn and bury her face in his chest, to cling to him like a child and confess her love for him. But she remained still, silent. To embarrass him with such a declaration would mean she would have to leave her job, the Rocking D, and the horses.

Leave Bart? The pain that tore through her at the

thought was almost physical, causing her to catch her bottom lip between her teeth. How could she leave him? Yet how could she stay here once Laina and he were married? The thoughts whirled around and around in her head. She could not decide now, she told herself. For now all she could do was will herself into some semblance of calm. Later, when he was gone, she would hash through all her thoughts. Consider the pros and cons. Come to some sane conclusion.

The filly nuzzled against Arabica's flank, began suckling noisily. Bart chuckled. "Greedy little thing."

"Yes." She hardly knew what she was saying.

"She'll get on," Bart continued. "The greedy ones reach out for what they want. That's the way to live. Take what you want from life."

Again Megan knew that searing pain. He was speaking of himself. She knew that. His advice did not apply to her. She had reached out. Last night she had given him everything of herself. Without thought see had offered herself.

Or perhaps, she thought bitterly, it was not she who had done the reaching at all. It was Bart who had reached out. Bart who had taken what he wanted. As he always had. As he always would.

"As Laina told you, we're leaving today for the rodeo circuit."

"Yes." She did not ask him why he had not mentioned this earlier. She had no right. Nor did she turn to face him.

"I only came home for your arrival and Arabica's delivery," he explained. "I don't know when I'll be back. I'll try to fly in from time to time and see how things are going."

She nodded. The hand that had been on her waist slipped down to rest on her hip. He acted, she thought, as if he owned her. But she did not draw away. She hadn't the strength to deny herself these few moments of contact with him.

"When I get back, we'll have our night," he said softly. "A *whole* night, like the one I meant us to have."

Her heart leaped high with hope while her head told her she could not do this thing. She couldn't let him any further into her heart.

He glanced down at his watch, then swung her toward him. "I have to go up to the house and get my stuff together. Pete'll be getting Dixie and the trailer ready."

She did not want to meet his eyes. Her own were swimming with unshed tears. Perhaps this was the last time she would see him. If she had any sense at all, she would leave the Rocking D before the rodeo season was over, before Bart returned to make her life a living hell.

But his gaze held hers. There was great tenderness in his eyes, great tenderness and warmth. And she fought hard to hide her feelings from him. But it appeared she was not successful.

"Hey, honey. Don't look so sad. The season doesn't last forever."

"I know." She managed to get the words out over the lump in her throat. For a moment she wondered again how Laina could put off marriage to this man. But perhaps love was different for her. Perhaps it did not mean this terrible need to touch and be touched, to hold and be held, to be an inseparable part of his life. But then, Laina *was* with him. And she could have all those things without benefit of marriage. For a time, at least.

He framed her face between calloused palms. "You have freckles," he said, his eyes traveling eagerly over her face.

"I've always had them," she said.

"I never noticed." He kissed one. "I like them."

Megan could not speak. She stood there paralyzed, her hands against his chest, his heart pulsing under her trembling fingers.

His eyes were warm and caressing. "I've just got time for one good kiss," he whispered. "Something to remember me by till I come back."

"I don't need—" Her protest was cut off in midsentence by his mouth covering hers. For a moment she considered fighting his kiss. But she knew it was useless. Her body was far stronger than her mind, and her need for him was overwhelming.

He lifted her entirely off her feet, clasping her to him with arms of steel. Her own arms crept around his neck, and she buried her hands in his hair. This, she thought, was their farewell kiss. And she opened her lips to him as she had opened her body the night before, offering herself for his possession.

The kiss was long and passionate. It left her light-headed and breathless, and when he set her once more on her feet she had to lean against him for support.

He groaned and buried his face in her hair. "Get out of here, honey. Go take a ride. Stay away till I'm gone. Otherwise . . ." He laughed softly. "I'll never get away on time."

"All right. Goodbye." She managed the words. She managed to get to the waiting mare and head her out away from the ranch. She even managed not to look back. But that was because the tears were streaming down her face and it would have been impossible to see him anyway.

As the mare moved obediently out onto the prairie, Megan tried to push Bart from her thoughts. She would seek out the stallion. Make friends with him. It would give her something to do, add some meaning to her life, she told herself bitterly. She must have some purpose to keep her going until she found another job, or saved enough to get away. But she would not think about leaving now, she told herself. The pain of it was too great.

Now she would think only of Diablo. Of how she might gentle him, accustom him to the sight of her. She would accomplish something during her stay here, she told herself defiantly. Something besides breaking her own foolish heart.

Chapter Eight

A week passed, then another. Every day found Megan on the west range, and every day brought the curious stallion closer. The first time he came close enough to sniff around, she felt almost heady with triumph. And when he took the sugar which she had left in the crown of her by-now dusty Stetson, she could have danced for joy.

She had been right in thinking that working with the stallion would help to allay her feelings for Bart. At least it filled her days.

The nights were another story. No matter how she exhausted herself, she had trouble sleeping. And, once asleep, she dreamed endlessly of Bart. Bart in church with Laina in white beside him. Bart on the big black stallion racing over the prairie. Bart being bucked off a saddle bronc and trampled.

And sometimes, Bart telling her that he loved her—her, Megan Ryan. It was these dreams that hurt the worst. For morning always dawned, bringing with it the knowledge that her joy had been false, that all she was to him was a good kid who deserved an evening out for her hard work.

Over and over she relived every moment with him: every look, every kiss, every caress. Every word he had said. But it was the words that pained the most, that shattered any dream castles she tried to build. He had said he wanted her. More than once he had said it. But never once had he mentioned love. And it was love that she needed from him. Love that she wanted with all her heart and soul.

She was thinking of this as she leaned against the corral fence, watching the filly Sunrise gambol about. Already the filly had filled out, losing some of the gangliness of the new born. A few days could make tremendous changes, Megan thought. But they had made no changes in her feelings for Bart. Except, perhaps, to intensify them.

A commotion in the stable yard made her raise her head as Pete came scurrying in. "It's the stallion," he said. "Some of the boys are bringing him. Looks like he run into some barbed wire."

Megan swung into action. "Put him in an empty box stall," she said. "I'll get my bag."

She could hear the stallion's frightened snorting and the curses of the cowhands as they worked to get him into the unfamiliar stable. Finally they were able to force him into the stall.

Megan, watching all this, wished she had had more time to work with him. All this snorting and plunging about would not help his injuries.

Panting, the men recoiled their ropes. "You can go now," Megan said. "I'll handle him."

She saw the frank disbelief in their eyes and knew that it was only their respect for her that kept them from laughing outright. No one was going to handle that stallion.

"Out," Megan repeated. "Your being here bothers him."

"But, miss—" One seemed about to voice a protest, but was quelled by her glance.

"Out. All of you," she repeated. "I'll handle this myself."

Silently the men filed out. But though not a word was said, their faces spoke eloquently. *Crazy fool woman. Has no business on a ranch.*

Pete watched the door close after the last man. "You got one of them tranquillizing guns?" he asked. "Put him to sleep?"

Megan shook her head. "That isn't necessary. Good-bye, Pete." She looked pointedly at the door.

"You can't go in there with that brute!" Pete's eyes bulged. "It's crazy. He'll stomp you."

Megan kept a firm hold on her anger. "Out, Pete. I'll call if I need you." When he didn't move, she added, "Go now, Pete. I can't attend to him while you're here. You make him nervous."

Pete went then, but his whole appearance made clear his dislike of the situation. This, his face said clearly, was not the way things should be done.

But Megan dismissed all that from her mind. Her main concern now was the horse. Through the bars of the stall, she surveyed him. He had stopped plunging about and was standing, watching her suspiciously. For the moment she ignored that, concentrating on his broad chest where two lines of ugly slashes showed the battle he had fought with the wire. The damage was rather widespread, Megan judged, but it didn't seem too deep. What she had to do now was calm him down. Those slashes needed to be cleaned and disinfected. Since the bleeding had already stopped they were probably not too bad.

She opened her bag and took out the necessary

items, stuffing them into her pockets. But she did not move immediately into the stall. First she took off her Stetson and, putting a lump of sugar in the crown, balanced it on the crossbars at the corner of the stall. She retreated slightly as the wary stallion advanced, snorting suspiciously. But he knew her scent, and, satisfied that she meant him no harm, he took the sugar cube neatly between his teeth.

Megan retrieved her hat and, with another lump of sugar reposing on its crown, held it before her as she advanced into the stall. She hummed softly as she moved toward him, hummed the same tune he had heard so often out on his home range.

She could still see the enlarged whites of his eyes and there were flecks of foam at the sides of his jaws, but he was watching her calmly. He took the proffered sugar, neatly, cleanly, between teeth that could inflict quite a painful wound. Megan set the Stetson back on her head and advanced a slow hand to the well-muscled neck. "Easy, boy," she crooned. "Easy does it." Her hands, gentle and swift, moved smoothly down to the gashed chest. Standing there, directly in front of the great horse, an easy target for his sharp hooves, she fished the disinfectant from her pocket and began to clean his wounds.

The box stall was a large one, meant to give its inhabitant moving room during a Montana winter. But though the stallion shifted from leg to leg nervously, he did not back away from her touch.

As she had suspected, the ugly gashes were not as bad as they looked. They were shallow, not deep. The beautiful black hide would be marred, perhaps, but no muscles or tendons had been damaged. If she could prevent infection, there should be no other problems.

The horse shifted his feet nervously and snorted, his head dipping into her hat as he searched for stray grains of sugar. Megan smiled. The techniques had worked. Diablo had learned to trust her.

"Easy, boy," she repeated, bending closer to inspect the long cut that curled down his leg. She knew the antiseptic must sting, but he accepted it, his nose still in her hat.

So intent was she on her work that she did not hear the approaching car. The slamming of the stable door startled both her and the horse. The stallion reared nervously and whinnied.

"Easy, boy." Megan reached high for the tossing head.

"Megan!" Bart's voice was heavy with fear. "Get the hell out of there. He'll trample you to shreds." He started toward the stall, and the stallion, getting his scent, began to plunge about.

"If he does, it'll be *your* fault," she called, her attention all on the horse. "Get out of here. Can't you see you're spooking him?"

"Megan! Please!"

"After I finish," she said calmly. "Now will you leave so I can?" She had one hand in the great horse's mane now and was crooning in his ear.

Bart cursed, loudly and profanely. But he retreated toward the door. "I'll be watching from the window," he cried. "If he goes for you, I'll shoot him."

"Don't be such an ass," Megan retorted, her frayed temper snapping under the strain. "You're the one who needs to be shot. I had this animal perfectly under control until you came butting in. Now get the hell out and let me finish my job!"

He left then, closing the door gently behind him, and Megan turned back to the fidgeting horse. "Don't worry about him, boy," she crooned softly. "It's just you and me now. And we know each other, don't we?"

The stallion snorted and nudged her shoulder, and

she reached up to put a hug around his neck. "You're a great horse, Diablo. Smart, too. Too bad you're not a man." She buried her face in the glossy neck. "At least you respond to love," she whispered, the hot tears rising. But she swallowed them and bent again to make sure the wounds were all clean. There seemed nothing more to be done at the moment, and she offered the stallion another sugar cube—this time on the palm of her hand.

He took it gently, the velvet of his muzzle just brushing her skin. Then, with another pat to his head, she let herself out of the stall, latching the door behind her. The stallion watched her for a moment and then, as she busied herself putting away her equipment, he turned away to his hay.

Megan heard the door open again, but she paid no attention. She didn't know if she could face him now. It hadn't been very smart to call the man names, especially where his ranch hands could hear. She had little doubt that her voice had carried to the cowboys waiting outside in eager clusters to see who would win the battle between the great stallion and the lady vet.

Everything was in place finally and Megan could fiddle with her kit no longer. She snapped it shut with a sigh, then straightened and turned. Though he had not said a word, she knew it was Bart who had entered. Her body had told her that clearly. She forced her features into a semblance of calm. "Hello. We didn't expect you back today."

His already glowering expression darkened as he glared at her. "I can see that. What the hell do you think you were doing in the stall with that brute?"

"Exactly what I was hired to do," she said calmly. "The stallion was injured, and I was cleaning the lacerations." Though she did not mean for them to do so, her eyes devoured him. He looked tired, she thought, the circles under his eyes were more pronounced, the lines in his face etched deeper.

He crossed the stable toward her, and she willed herself not to retreat. He was angry, angrier even than he had been that morning on the prairie. "You little fool! I told you to stay away from that horse."

She faced him squarely. "Unless he needed care," she reminded him. "And he did."

His expression did not lighten. "You didn't have to get in the stall with him. One wrong move and he'd have killed you."

"Don't be silly." She tried to reach down deep within herself, to tap some pool of anger, find something to distract her mind—and her body—from the man who stood so close to her.

His hands shot out suddenly, grabbing her upper arms in a vise-like grip. "Don't push me too far," he snapped. "I know that horse. He tried to kill me. He hates people."

Megan met his gaze fearlessly. "He hates *men*," she corrected. "Because they've hurt and abused him. He trusts me."

Bart's eyes narrowed. "And how did that trust develop so quickly?" he asked.

Megan shrugged, though his grip on her arms made it difficult. "I don't know. I suppose he can tell I don't mean to hurt him."

Bart snorted. "Am I supposed to buy that?"

By now she was sure his grip on her arms would leave ugly bruises. "I don't find it so farfetched. Horses know when we're afraid of them. Why shouldn't they sense other things? Anyway," she added defiantly, "I don't really care what you think. I came to the Rocking D to do a job. And I'm going to do it whether you like it or not!"

This last bit of defiance caused him to tighten his

grip until her arms ached. "You're a stupid foolish girl!" he shouted.

"Woman!" The word was wrenched from her. "I'm a woman!" she repeated. "And you know it."

Something gleamed in his eyes then, something wild and wicked. "That's not something I'm likely to forget," he cried. "But that only makes it worse. You've no business messing around with that devil. He could kill you that quick."

"But he won't." Megan put all she could into her pleading glance. "You've got to understand. Please, Bart!"

His face was so set that she wondered if he had heard anything she said. His eyes were hard, glittering like chunks of blue ice, and the grip on her arms tightened until she could not prevent herself from crying out at the pain of it.

The hard look vanished as his hands fell away and he seemed to come back to the present. Megan rubbed automatically at her numbed arms, not knowing that for a moment he had seen her slender body trampled and bleeding beneath the stallion's striking hooves.

"I was in no danger," she told him again. "Diablo trusts me."

His jaw hardened. "I don't know *how* you did it," he said. "But in the future you stay away from that stallion. Treat him from *outside* the stall. And that's an order!"

"Yes, sir!" She snapped out the reply, hoping that he wouldn't read in her eyes that she didn't mean to obey it. In all fairness she supposed that he had a point. But so did she. And he had refused to see it.

He continued to glare down at her, but she felt her anger begin to ebb. The scar above his eyes was a thin angry line. Her fingers ached to touch it, to smooth away the heavy lines of worry that corrugated his forehead. To gather his hard body against her own softness and give him all the love and comfort that welled up within her whenever she looked at his tired face. With an effort, she pushed these thoughts down again. She could never be to him what she wanted to be. He would not let her. "If there is nothing else," she said, all anger gone from her voice, "I'll put my things away."

For long moments he did not answer her, his eyes probing hers. She felt herself drawn toward him; the very cells of her body were pulled toward his. Her hands ached to touch him, her breasts ached to feel his flesh. Deep within her longing twisted and yearned. She wanted him; she wanted him fiercely, so fiercely that she had to dig her nails into her palms to keep her hands from reaching out to him. God, such wanting as she had never imagined. And still she stood, silent, calm, presenting him with a face that betrayed nothing.

Finally he spoke. "That'll be all. But mind what I said, Megan. Keep away from that stallion! Or else!"

She did not reply to his threat, simply bent to pick up her bag and walked slowly past him toward the tack room. She supposed it was his stupid male pride that made him so harsh. His ego was bruised because she had gentled the horse. His image of himself as a big macho man had been tarnished, and that bothered him. Still, she told herself as she put her bag on the shelf, it was a small defeat for him.

Once back on the circuit he would be admired by hundreds of young pretty girls, girls who were willing to do just about anything for a handsome cowboy. And of course, if that palled, there was always Laina. Angry again, Megan shut the door, barely catching it in time to prevent its banging from being heard in the other room. But she needn't have been so careful, for when she returned to the stable it was empty, there was no sign of Bart anywhere.

The stable yard, however, was full of hands, and Megan forced herself to walk out there. This was not the time or the place for the tears she felt like shedding. They would have to wait for the privacy of her bedroom that night, she thought as she stepped into the sunlight.

"I never seen the like of it," chortled Pete, his wrinkled face exuberant. "You got that old stallion eating right outa your hand. Tell us, Megan, how'd you do it?"

She was surrounded by eager, friendly faces, and Megan smiled. "It's not so hard, really. I let the horse get used to me. Let him learn to trust me. That's all."

"That's all!" repeated a cowboy, his grin wide. "Not only does she tame the damnedest meanest critter this side of the Rockies, but she calls the boss an—"

"That's enough," said Pete, and his eyes held a threat that kept the cowhand silent. "I reckon there's work to be done on this ranch."

Megan flushed as she recalled again the way she had talked to Bart. But he had brought it on himself. He was so stubborn, so obstinate. Never listening to reason. Never understanding her. How could he expect her to treat the animals if he didn't let her near them? But then, there was no reasoning with men like Bart. They thought they knew everything. And acted like it.

Finally the cowhands dispersed, helped on their way by a couple of hard glances from Pete. Megan turned away, wondering where she could go so as not to run into Bart again.

"Megan." Pete's tone was so strange she swung on her heel to face him.

"What, Pete?"

"Got a minute?" he asked with a sober face.

"Sure, Pete. What is it?"

He cast a look around him. "C'mon inside."

"Sure." Megan followed him into the tack room's coolness and settled down on a stool. "What's so secret?"

"I know you got yer reasons," Pete said, carefully avoiding her eyes. "And the boss can be pretty rough sometimes." He squinted at her shrewdly. "But you'd best have a care. He's a man, you know. And he's got his pride."

Megan felt the blood rush to her face. Not by word or look had Pete ever referred to that evening she had spent in Billings with Bart. But something in his look told her he was thinking of it now.

"What did I do so wrong?" she asked. "I only wanted to treat the horse."

Pete shook his head. "I know the boss can be provoking. Nobody knows that better'n me. But you can't go round yelling at him like that. 'Specially in front of the boys. He's got his pride." He scratched thoughtfully at his grizzled head. "A little bit of a thing like you. And that great beast. The whole county'll know about it afore nightfall."

Megan scrambled to her feet. "I don't know what I can do about it, Pete. The horse was hurt. He needed to be cared for. And Bart came roaring in like that and spooked him. So I lost my temper." She smiled ruefully. "I'm not perfect, you know. And I've had my share of tension, too."

Pete's face was sympathetic. "I know, lass. I see more'n I let on. I'm just trying to give you warning. The boss ain't no man to mess around with."

"I know, Pete. I know. I'll try to watch my step."

"That's all I wanted from you." He pulled out his pocket knife and began to whittle. "You're a smart girl. You'll learn."

Megan, wrestling the saddle onto Darling's back, wondered rather dismally what she was supposed to learn. No matter how much she catered to Bart's masculine ego, she would never have the chance to gain his love. Perhaps he was unable to love, she thought as she swung up into the saddle and headed out toward the range. But that was not going to help her any. She wanted his love. Wanted it more desperately than she had ever wanted anything in her life.

Chapter Nine

❧

It was getting dark when Megan and the mare reentered the stable yard. If she was lucky, Bart would be gone by now, doubtless spending the evening with Laina, Megan told herself. If she had come home with him.

She dismounted heavily, feeling as though she were a hundred years old. Absently she rubbed the mare's soft nose. This time when Bart left she would have to do some hard thinking. It seemed impossible to go on the way they were. But to leave here, to never see Bart again, seemed even worse. She doubted that she could bring herself to do it.

She put the mare into her stall and went to put the saddle away, bringing the currycomb and brush back with her. As always, grooming a horse brought its own comfort. How many times in her youth had she retreated to the horsy warmth of the barn to battle her way through seemingly insurmountable problems. Somehow she had survived everything that life had thrown at her, she thought as her hands worked automatically. And she would survive this, too. She must.

She worked quietly there in the stable's soft light, no sound but the comfortable noise of horses chomping on hay and the rustle of straw as they moved about their stalls. Finally a small measure of peace crept into her heart. There was some way out of this, she told herself firmly. And she would find it.

She returned the currycomb and brush to the tack room and went to make her usual nightly rounds. It had become something of a habit for her these last two weeks to check on the mare and filly before she went in for the night, as well as any other animal that was ailing. Now, of course, she would add the stallion to the list. She patted her pocket to be sure she had some sugar left, then moved off across the stable.

Arabica had become a model mother, Megan told herself as she leaned on the railing watching the filly nurse. Motherhood had come so easily to the mare. As it would to her, said a voice in her head, if only the child were Bart's. She shook her head, trying to dislodge the painful image, but it remained. She wanted Bart Dutton's child. She wanted it badly. But she wanted it as a token of love—mutual love, not just her love—and that could never be.

Slowly she straightened and went on to the stall where the stallion stood. He was watching her approach, but he didn't seem at all wary. In fact, he stuck his head over the top pole and whickered at her in greeting. Megan grinned. It was impossible to be completely downhearted when she considered her success with Diablo. He had restored her faith. In what, she was not quite sure. And then the truth hit home.

Diablo had restored her faith in love. For it was love that she had offered him out there on the prairie. A love based on trust and respect. And he had accepted it. If only humans . . . She brushed the thought aside. Enough of that kind of thinking. She was here to examine the stallion's wounds. To see that everything was in order.

Rubbing the soft nose extended to her, she spoke to him affectionately. "You've got to let me look at you first. That's a good boy." Mindful of Bart's orders, she crouched down, trying to get a good look at the horse's chest from between the boards of the stall. But the stallion was eager for his sugar and pressed against the stall, trying to reach the hat which had so often held treats for him.

Straightening, Megan laughed and pushed his head aside. "Not yet, silly. You have to let me look at you." She cast a quick glance around, her lip curling in irritation. Bart was being impossible. There was no way she could check the wounds without getting in the stall. If he found her there, Bart would be very angry. But she knew she was in no danger. The great horse would never hurt her. Besides, it was just about dinnertime. With any luck, if he was on the ranch at all, Bart would be eating.

She straightened her shoulders and decided to risk it. In a very few minutes she could see what she needed to see. Then she would be out again and Bart none the wiser. Lifting the latch, she opened the door and stepped in. Diablo moved toward her eagerly, whuffling in anticipation. Megan smoothed the great neck. "Hold on, boy. Just let me see."

He stood obediently while she bent to examine his chest. Everything seemed all right, she thought as the horse bent and nuzzled her shoulder with velvet-soft lips.

Megan straightened with a sigh. "I love you, too," she said. "But I'm afraid we'd better keep it a—"

The squeak of the opening door alerted her, and she cast about her for some place to hide, even while she knew that such an effort was useless.

"Megan? Are you in here?"

It was Bart, as she had known it would be, and she answered him, her voice low and clear, knowing instinctively that he would not come this far without checking in the stalls. "I'll be right there," she called, injecting her voice with a cheerfulness she was far from feeling.

She heard the hiss of his indrawn breath and knew that he had determined her whereabouts. She gave the stallion another pat and turned to unlatch the door. It was her intent, by her leisurely departure from the stallion's box, to show Bart how gentled the horse had become. Surely he would not continue to resent her having tamed him.

But as she reached for the latch the door opened and a long arm reached in and literally yanked her out. Megan's gasp of outrage alerted the stallion, who advanced toward the intruder with bared teeth. Bart, slamming the door in his face, threw Megan to one side into the straw and rolled after her.

For a moment she lay there, stunned by the quick turn of events. Then she gathered her scattered wits and tried to scramble to her feet.

But he would not let her. He grabbed one booted ankle and sent her sprawling, then threw himself on top of her. Megan pounded futilely on his back with her small fists. "Let me up! Let me go!"

"No!" The word was abrupt and final. He enforced it with the weight of his body. She felt him pressing on her, his hard thighs against hers, his belt buckle digging into her stomach. "You're not going anywhere until I say so."

She stopped struggling then; it was so clearly useless.

"What do you want from me?" The words were half a sob.

"Some common sense," he snarled. The light above him cast his face into the shadow, but she could see the cruel twist to his mouth. "I told you to stay out of the stallion's stall. He could have killed you!"

Megan felt the sudden tears spilling over. "That's a bold-faced lie!" She spat the words at him. "He would never hurt me. It was you he was after. Because you hurt me. Let me up and I'll show you." She struggled against him.

His fingers dug cruelly into the tender flesh of her shoulders. "You'll do no such thing."

Megan felt suddenly exhausted. She yearned for the comfort he could provide her. The hard male body that now pinned her to the straw could cover her with tenderness, with longing. She heard the increase of his breath, felt the stirring of his maleness against her leg, and panic overtook her. If she yielded to him now, here in the hay like any common . . . She could not even think the word. She would never forgive herself. Desperately she sought for some way to escape him. She could not use physical weapons; she would have to resort to verbal ones.

"I'm sorry I wounded the great man's pride," she taunted. "But the truth of the matter is, I've tamed your devil stallion. Anyone could have done it, of course." She babbled on, watching the anger mount on his face. "Anyone with a little sense. But of course, you—"

"That's enough," he cried, crushing his lips against hers, Megan tasted blood where her lip had been caught between her teeth. Savagely he ground his mouth against hers, obliterating all her efforts to resist him. Her flailing fists were pinned above her head and his body ground against hers until she thought she would pass out because her lungs could get no air. He ravaged her mouth, and she knew that her body would be next. The anger she had provoked in him, anger designed to distract him, had not served its purpose. Instead, it had driven him deeper into this vengeful sexuality.

One hand slid down to her shirtfront. She fought him with all her strength. Any second now he would rip the clothes from her body. The stallion, sensitive to her distress, whickered nervously and began to kick at the stall as Bart's hand closed roughly over one heaving breast. Any second now he would do it. She closed her eyes and waited.

And then came the creak of the door and Pete's voice, like that of a savior, floating into the room. "Bart, there's a phone call. Long distance."

Megan felt the body that held hers slowly relax. "Be right there, Pete. Tell them to hold on."

"Okay."

Megan lay still, her eyes closed, afraid to move for fear Bart would renew his assault. But Pete's voice had broken the spell. When Bart spoke, his tone was even. "Open your eyes," he said.

She did not think of disobeying. The blue eyes probed hers. "You hear me now, Megan Ryan. I mean what I say. Keep away from that stallion. If you don't—" He glared at her menacingly. "You'll be sorry. Understand?"

Megan nodded. Under the circumstances it was foolish to do anything else.

"Good." He heaved himself to his feet and stood there, towering over her, hands planted on hips. "You've had a busy day. I think you ought to go to bed early. Now, in fact."

Then he was gone, the stable lights throwing his shadow before him.

Megan waited till the door had closed behind him before she moved. The nerve of the man, treating her like that. Sending her to bed—like a naughty child. And without any supper, too!

She got stiffly to her feet and made her way through the tack room to the little room she dignified by the name of office. In the cracked mirror that hung there she got a good look at herself. Her skin had turned a honey gold from the sun, but it did not hide the shadows under her eyes or the pain that seemed to linger in their velvet depths.

Love was certainly a fearful thing, she told herself, as she found a clean tissue and wiped away the blood on her lip. This was a love so fearful that it made her quake inside. It was not love, of course, that made Bart behave as he did, but wounded male pride. But it was love that kept her here—chained to this place by love for a man who felt nothing but rage toward her.

She examined her face carefully, pulled a comb through the auburn hair, and set out toward the kitchen. She would go to bed, all right, glad to avoid his company. But she had no intention of going there on an empty stomach. If Mrs. Grean wasn't about, she would raid the refrigerator and take her chances.

But Mrs. Grean was still in the kitchen, stirring up something delectable for the next day. She greeted Megan with a big smile, and if her sharp eyes noted the cut lip, she made no comment. "So there you are, lass. You've got to stop this missing of meals," she scolded good-naturedly. "It's not good for a body at all."

"I know, Mrs. Grean." Megan was too tired to argue. "It's just that today the stallion was hurt—and then I was riding. And, well . . ." She made a half-hearted gesture with her hands. "You know how it is."

"Yes, I do. And I know all about that stallion, too, the terrible beast. And Mr. Bart fit to be tied 'cause of the chances you was taking. I never seen him in such a rage before."

Megan debated about giving Mrs. Grean the true facts. That it wasn't danger to her that put Bart in such a vile humor. It was damage to his male pride. But she didn't think Mrs. Grean would believe anything bad about Bart. Whenever she spoke of him, everything about her announced that she thought the man a wonder.

She took a seat at the heavy table. "I know I'm late," she said, giving the housekeeper a rueful smile. "But do you have anything I can eat?"

Mrs. Grean's snort was pronounced. "There's never been a time I couldn't find something in my kitchen for a body to eat. You just sit still and have this nice cup of coffee." And she set a steaming mug in front of Megan.

"Thank you, Mrs. Grean." Megan wrapped her hands around the cup. The August evening wasn't cool, but she felt somehow chilled. Her encounter with Bart had shaken her to the core. How angry he must have been to want to punish her in that age-old way. She shivered slightly, thinking of what she had so fortunately escaped.

"Here you go," said Mrs. Grean, putting a big bowl of vegetable soup and a plate of sourdough biscuits in front of her.

Megan sniffed appreciatively. "It smells just wonderful," she said, reaching for her spoon. "It's homemade, of course." And she met the older woman's eyes. "And homemade biscuits with butter! I couldn't ask for a better meal."

"The whole did turn out well," the housekeeper

agreed complacently. "But then, it's a God-given gift, I have. So 'tis hardly fair for me to be taking the credit for it."

Megan smiled. Mrs. Grean's sane comfortable company was beginning to restore her to a feeling of normalcy. The dark shadow side of Bart that she had glimpsed seemed to fade. Of course, he had been angry, very angry. And perhaps he had not intended what she thought he had. Perhaps he would have come to himself without Pete's timely interference.

As she finished up her soup, she felt a great wave of fatigue sweeping over her. She wanted only to go to bed, to welcome the oblivion of sleep and the release, however temporary, that it gave her.

She shook her head at the slice of apple pie that the housekeeper offered her. "Not tonight. I'm sure it's delicious. I'm just full."

Mrs. Grean's forehead puckered with worry. "I hope you aren't coming on to catch something. You've been looking mighty peaked lately. Don't eat enough to keep a bird alive."

This last brought a tired smile from Megan. "I promise you. I'll turn over a new leaf. From now on I'll eat like a horse. Two horses."

The housekeeper sniffed, but she returned Megan's smile. "More'n likely it'll be like two birds."

Megan joined in the laughter, then got wearily to her feet. "If Bart asks for me, tell him I've gone to bed."

"I will if I see him," said the housekeeper, her face strangely sober. "He's gone over to the Darwoods, so I suppose he'll not be in till late."

Megan nodded, carefully controlling her expression. So Bart had run off to Laina after their quarrel; no doubt he would give her some distorted version of the truth. And because she loved him, she would believe it.

With a sigh Megan trudged up the stairs. Her feet

felt as heavy as her heart, she thought as she dragged herself along the hall to her room. He was very angry with her now, very angry. And there was no way to redeem herself in his eyes. No way at all.

Chapter Ten

When Megan went to breakfast the next day, Bart was gone. Back to the circuit, Mrs. Grean told her. He had left very early after conferring with Pete, so the housekeeper said.

Megan nodded. It didn't take much thinking to guess what they had conferred about. And when she went out to the stables to check the horses, she knew she'd been right. Diablo had been returned to the range.

She saw Pete eyeing her, wondering, no doubt, what her reaction would be. And for his sake she said, "He should have been kept here another day or two. I suppose it was Bart's orders that he be turned loose."

Pete nodded. "You give that man quite a skeer. I ain't never seen him so angry before."

"And all for nothing," Megan replied coolly. "That stallion would never hurt me."

Pete shook his head. "I'm some inclined to believe you after the things I seen. But you're fergetting something important. Bart's been under that critter's hooves.

And Diablo weren't fooling none. You seen that scar on his forehead."

Megan nodded.

"Well, then, ain't it sort of natural he should be afraid for you?"

Megan sighed. "I suppose so," she conceded. "But it's still ridiculous. The stallion's been mistreated by men. No wonder he hates them. But he likes me. I'd trust my life with him."

Pete frowned. "You done that every time you stepped into his stall. Ain't a man on the circuit would have done that."

Megan threw up her hands in disgust. "There's no use talking to either one of you. You don't listen worth a damn!"

"Temper! Temper!" said Pete, his eyes twinkling at her.

Megan's anger left as quickly as it had come. "I'm Irish, too, you know. I've got my share of temper."

"That ain't no news to me," replied Pete.

Megan gathered up her gear. "I'm going for a ride," she said. "See you later."

Pete opened his mouth as though he was about to say something, then closed it sharply. But Megan would have bet that he'd been about to warn her away from the west range. She headed Darling east, conscious that Pete's eyes were upon. But eventually the lay of the land would hide her from him and then she would turn west. If Bart Dutton thought he could keep her from Diablo like this, he had another think coming.

The sun was hot as Megan finally approached the waterhole, and she wished she had brought a canteen. The great stallion was not in sight, but she let Darling have a cool drink, then hitched her to a shady tree. With a sigh Megan stretched out under another. She was finding it increasingly difficult to rest at night, tossing and turning until the sheets were all twisted and still not getting any sleep. But out here she found it easier to relax. She would just close her eyes and listen for Diablo.

Megan was wakened from a sound sleep by something pushing her Stetson off her face. She felt something soft brush her cheek and opened her eyes to find Diablo's nose only inches from her own.

"Hello, fella." Megan reached up to give him a pat. "Wouldn't Bart have a fit if he could see us now."

The stallion twitched his tail and moved around to nuzzle her jeans. Megan laughed. "You know where the sugar is, don't you?" She pushed herself to her knees and turned to face him. "But first I want to see your chest. Easy now."

The great horse stood quietly while Megan examined him. The cuts seemed to be healing nicely, and his return to the open range shouldn't harm him. But it meant more riding for Megan, for now she needed the great horse's companionship.

When finally she pulled herself away from him, another idea had formed in her mind. Now, if she could only get a bridle out of the tack room without anyone missing it, she bet anything Diablo would let her up on him, would let her ride him even. At least it was something to think about, something to take her mind off Bart and his anger.

Smuggling the bridle out of the tack room and into her saddlebag turned out to be easier than she thought. She just waited till Pete and the other cowhands were at lunch.

So the next morning when Diablo came for his sugar, Megan had a bridle for him to sniff, and before she left the west range that day she had had it over his head.

The third morning dawned bright and clear. Megan awoke with a feeling of expectancy. This was the morning she meant to mount Diablo. She had considered Bart's commands, but she could not obey them. Something within her cried out to ride the great horse. In some way that was not clear to her, the horse had become her connection with Bart. When she was with the stallion, she missed Bart less. There was no logic to it, since even being near the horse was directly contrary to Bart's express wishes, but still Megan went. It was only out there on the west range with Diablo beside her that she felt any hope for the future. Out there she didn't think of the insurmountable problems that faced her, or even of the fact that she was disobeying Bart.

Out there she only used her senses. She felt the warm sun on her face, the stallion's glossy coat under her fingers, the cool water of the stream running over bare feet. She smelled the pungent sage, the sun-baked earth, the clean scent of Diablo's hide. She gazed at the prairie, filling herself with the sight of the blue sky, the rolling land, the green cottonwoods. She tasted the wind, soft on her tongue, the tepid water of her canteen, the sweet grains of sugar. Even her ears were more alert, though aside from the sounds she and the horses generated, the prairie offered nothing more than the occasional far cry of a meadowlark, and a profound silence.

It was that silence, she thought, that must have gotten to the first settlers. How many pioneer wives had found it impossible to bear?

Megan stretched and pushed back the covers. Diablo was awaiting her. But when she reached the kitchen, she discovered that her great day must be postponed.

Mrs. Grean looked up from her pastry and said, "Pete says you should get some clothes together soon as you eat breakfast. Bart wants the pilot to fly you out to Browning."

Megan felt for a second that her heart had stopped beating. She finally managed to get the words out. "To Browning? What for?"

"He told Pete that Dixie has something wrong with her leg. You know he's been entering the calf roping these past few years. It ain't as hard on the bones." The housekeeper shook her head. "I sure do wish he'd retire from saddle-bronc riding. Why, he ain't got an arm or a leg left that ain't been broke. Anyway"—with one deft motion she flipped a pie shell into the waiting pan—"Pete said to tell you to get ready."

"Of course." Megan didn't quite know how to feel. She knew that she wanted to see Bart, even though it was not a wise thing to do. But he was probably still mad at her. And what if . . . She pushed the thought away. Bart was the boss. If he said fly to Browning, then that's what she would do.

She ate the breakfast Mrs. Grean set before her without tasting a bite, then went upstairs and packed a suitcase. No silk dress and wispy sandals this time, she thought grimly. This time the trip was really business. Her suitcase packed, she carried it downstairs, then went out to check her bag. It was too bad he hadn't been more specific about Dixie. She might have had a better idea what to take along.

Pete came into the tack room just as she emerged from her office, bag in hand. "I'm ready," she said evenly.

"Good." Pete's expression was rather strange, and Megan wondered if he was thinking of that two-a.m. call to Billings. "I'll drive you out to the airfield."

Megan nodded. "What did he tell you about Dixie?" she asked.

Pete shrugged. "Didn't say much. Just that she's favoring her right leg and he wants you to look at it."

"Surely there must be a vet around there." She knew that if he was thinking of Billings, this was not the right comment to make, but nevertheless she felt compelled to say it.

Pete shrugged again. "Reckon the boss wanted his own vet. After all, you're on salary."

"But the cost of flying . . ."

Pete's eyes narrowed shrewdly, but his expression didn't change. "The plane's paid fer. And the pilot's on salary."

"Still . . ."

"He wants you," Pete said, in a tone that brooked no argument. "And he's the boss."

"Yes," said Megan, her voice carrying more than a hint of sarcasm. "So I've been told."

This time Megan did not sleep in the plane. She watched the landscape unroll beneath them. Even from the air the prairie seemed huge, sprawling like some giant. As the plane circled before touching down on the little landing field outside of Browning, Megan's heart rose up in her throat. But it was not from fear of the ground that seemed to be rising up to meet them, but from knowing that somewhere down there Bart Dutton was waiting for her. And she did not know how she was going to behave.

The plane rolled slowly to a stop, and Megan, wiping her hands nervously on her jeans, peered out the small window. A rented car was parked beside the field, and next to it she spied a tall figure. Although she could not see the face beneath the Stetson, she knew from the prickling of her skin that it was Bart Dutton who stood there.

Minutes later he was opening the door, extending a

brown hand to help her descend. She laid her own in it
with a feeling of trepidation, knowing that his touch
would send her body into tremors of longing that could
not be denied.

"Hello, Megan." His voice was deep, almost a
caress. "How are you?"

"I'm fine, thank you," she replied, feeling a little
foolish at this formality, hoping that her expression did
not reveal how much she had been longing for the sight
of him. He looked tired, she thought, her eyes making
a quick assessment. And when he bent to pick up her
case, he limped slightly.

"You've been hurt," she said, unable to keep the
anxiety from her voice.

He shrugged. "Just an old injury acting up. It must
be going to rain."

More words rose to Megan's lips, but she swallowed
them. He would not take kindly to being clucked over
by a mother hen.

"What seems to be the matter with Dixie?" she
asked as he helped her in the car and set the case in
the back.

"Can't tell exactly." His expression did not change.
"Seems to be favoring her right front leg. Didn't want
to take any chances. I paid a good sum for her, you
know. Good roping horses don't come cheap."

Megan nodded. "I brought my bag."

"Good. I thought we'd go directly to the arena. Let
you look at her right away."

"That sounds good." Megan felt as if she were two
women. One was sitting here making polite conversa-
tion about a horse while the other was fighting for control of her body. She clasped the bag with both hands.
If only she could touch him, reach out just for one
brief caress. But of course she couldn't. This was
strictly a business trip, and she had to keep it that way.

"How's the stallion?" he asked conversationally.

"I expect he's fine." This was one answer Megan had prepared. "I did think you returned him to the range a little soon. But then, you're the boss."

Bart cast her a look of speculation at this, but she managed to keep her features expressionless. He was not going to trap her into admitting that she had been with the stallion. She had made up her mind to that.

"He'll survive. He's tough enough, the brute."

Megan contented herself with a nod. But she couldn't refrain from an inner smile. If he had any idea how the "brute" followed her about like a big dog, grazed right beside her while she slept—now that would really have made him yell.

The streets around the arena were beginning to fill up with cars full of people eager to see the rodeo. Megan was aware of a rising excitement. Although she had seen televised rodeo events, she had never attended a real performance.

She was so busy gazing around her that she wasn't sure how Bart got to the stables. But soon he was stopping the car and helping her out. He took her bag in one hand and, clasping her hand with the other, set off through the crowds, drawing her after him.

Some minutes later they stood before the stall that held Bart's mare. On seeing Megan, she stuck her head over the top of the stall and whickered a greeting.

Bart gave Megan a strange glance. "Don't tell me she remembers you," he exclaimed.

"I'm not telling you anything," Megan said quietly. "Hello, girl. How are you?"

She rubbed the mare's silky neck. "Let me come in and take a look at you." Suiting her actions to her words, she slipped inside the stall. She tried to blot Bart's presence from her mind as she ran her fingers gently over the mare's leg. She could detect no swelling, no sprain, no injury to a tendon. She lifted the mare's foot and inspected the hoof. Sometimes the simplest thing could be overlooked. But there was nothing lodged under the mare's shoe.

Megan straightened. "I don't see anything. Did she slip or stumble?"

Bart shook his head. "No. I just noticed that she seemed to be favoring it."

Megan frowned. "Sorry. I just don't see anything."

"Why don't I show you your room?" Bart said. "It's close. You can settle in and then come watch. Ever see a rodeo before?"

"No. Only on TV." Megan avoided his eyes. She was not sure she wanted to watch him perform.

"Then this'll be a treat for you," he said, and, hand in the small of her back, he guided her again to the car, where he retrieved her suitcase. "It's only a couple blocks. With traffic like this it's easier to walk."

Megan nodded. She tried to concentrate on the sights around her, tried not to look at Bart, not to think of him on a saddle bronc or lying in the arena dirt being trampled while she was up in the stands unable to reach him.

Bart took her straight to the door of her room and handed her the key. Then he reached into his pocket for a ticket. "Compliments of the house," he said, grinning.

There was nothing for her to do but accept it. "Thank you."

Almost as though he sensed her reluctance, he spoke again. "I'll be looking for you. Okay?"

"Okay." Megan dropped her eyes. He was standing too close now. She caught his male smell, and desire rose deep within her. She almost leaned toward him, so intense was her need for him. For the merest moment she thought that he might gather her in his arms, but he did not. And she remained standing so, until he said, "See you later then," and walked away.

Chapter Eleven

❧

The rodeo was exciting, Megan had to admit that. The seat Bart had given her was a very good one, with a great view of the arena. Sitting there, surrounded by laughing, talking people, she wondered how many of them were watching those they loved. And how many were there just for the thrills and excitement.

There was no doubt that it was thrilling. The very air reeked with excitement. This kind of thing was strange to her. She understood the desire to win, to demonstrate skill—which was certainly a part of competition. What she could not get a hold on was the deliberate courting of danger and injury. Of course, no one *wanted* to get hurt. Yet they knew the odds that they would were quite high. A saddle-bronc rider, as Pete had explained it to her, was considered really lucky to escape injury for even a single season. And a bull rider fared even worse.

The broncs, of course, did not often try to stomp and trample a fallen rider. Diablo was an exception there. Usually bucking horses were quite gentle, were halter-broken and could be easily led. It was only when they were mounted that they went into their bucking acts. The ride over, they headed back for the corral.

But the bulls were a different story. Mean and vicious, some of them, with big horns that could put a hole through a man in a minute. Megan shivered. She would never consider getting into a stall with one of those brutes.

Diablo was not like that, she thought, wondering if he had missed her that morning. Well, it wouldn't be long and she'd be out on the range with him again. Her legs ached in anticipation of the great rides they would have. As long as Bart stayed on the circuit. By the time the season was over, she would have the great stallion for a pet. She knew it.

The hiss of indrawn breath in a thousand throats pulled her attention back to the arena. Another bull rider had hit the dirt, and this bull was out to get him. Megan held her breath as the clowns moved swiftly to distract the great beast. One clown, who kept poking his head out of the barrel, looked as if he was going to get hit, but withdrew his head just in time.

Megan smiled. Although she had never been to an actual rodeo before, her love of horses had led her to read a great deal about them. At first she'd been surprised to discover that bucking horses were bred for that purpose and could become champions just as the cowboys could.

But she had been most amazed by the clowns. They earned no points, got no championships. Yet year after year they went on, risking their lives to keep the riders safe. Megan relaxed now as the downed cowboy scampered to safety up the pole fence and the bull finally retreated back into the arena.

Watching the bull riders was exciting, Megan thought, but it was not as though she knew any of the men out there. Most of them were young, some still in their teens. The rodeo business was a young man's game, she told herself. But then cowboys, real cowboys in the long-ago days, had been very young, much younger than the movies usually portrayed them. The life that the rodeo events had evolved from had been a strenuous life, rising early to settle a bucking horse before breakfast, then long hard hours out in the elements.

The announcer's voice brought Megan back to the present. "Saddle-bronc riding, ladies and gents. And we've got some great riders for you. World champions, some of them. All out there to get a chance at that prize money."

Megan watched as a rider eased himself down onto the restless bronc. She found her palms had gone sweaty. Suddenly the chute opened and the horse came rocketing out, the cowboy spurring hard.

Dear God, Megan thought, how can the human body endure such terrible jolting? She watched closely, trying to see the things Pete had told her about saddle-bronc riding. How the rider had to keep one hand in the air, how he was supposed to spur, with his toes pointed out, have the spurs over the bronc's shoulders and touching the horse when the bronc's feet touched the ground first jump out of the chute. The time whistle shrilled through the air, and the cowboy's hand came down quickly to grab the saddle as he struggled to keep his seat till the pickup man got to him.

Megan began computing possible points in her mind.

A big beefy man to the right of her pushed back his hat, rubbed one hand across his sweaty forehead, and turned to the woman next to him. "Not a bad ride," he said. "But that there's a union horse if I ever saw one."

The woman nodded. "Yeah. He quit soon as the whistle blew."

Megan smiled. She liked the West's down-to-earth expressions. She tried to recall an expression Pete had used, something about a cowboy's shining his boots if he pointed his toes in instead of out during his ride.

As the cowboy moved out of the arena, the announcer spoke again. "And now, Bart Dutton, coming out of chute number three. On old Thunderbolt." The rest of the announcer's words were lost as Megan's eyes went to the chute. She could see Bart, his blue-checked shirt damp from his exertions, easing himself down on the plunging horse. Then suddenly the horse disappeared from view—and with him Bart. Megan was on her feet instantly, her heart in her mouth. It was only with the greatest effort that she stopped herself from elbowing past the beefy man and his wife and trying to find her way into the arena.

Then the announcer's voice broke into her agonized thoughts. "He's okay, folks. Bart Dutton was down, but he's up now. Looking okay."

Megan's breath came out in a great sigh of relief. Thank God he was safe. She watched as his head emerged above the poles of the chute. He dusted off his Stetson, clamped it tightly on again, and resumed his seat.

Her knees weak, she sank down. She could never stand being married to a rodeo man, she thought. The tension would be too much for her, always wondering if this was the day he'd be hurt. And if a woman didn't go to the events, didn't watch, it would be even worse. Then she would be waiting for the phone to ring or for his friends to drive up to give her the bad news.

Megan forced herself to sit still, to watch as the gate opened and Bart's bronc came out of the chute. She tried to be objective about the whole thing. The horse was performing well—kicking high, lunging and spinning, even sunfishing. Bart's form was excellent. His feet moved rhythmically in the stirrups; his balance showed he had the feel of the animal. He was making a very good ride, she thought, if only he could stay the whole eight seconds. Just then the whistle blew and Megan sagged with relief as he reached back to release the flank strap. One more ride over and no injuries.

Bart leaned toward the pickup horse as it drew near and slid easily to the ground. His smile acknowledged the crowd's cheers and whistles as the announcer gave him a high score. But his eyes were searching the stands, searching for her. Megan's heart threatened to stop beating when they found her. Even over that distance she could feel the warmth in his glance. Then he raised his Stetson gaily and blew her a kiss off one dusty palm.

The crowd went wild. Megan felt the blood rising to her face at the thought of acknowledging his gesture in front of all these people. But his gaze continued to hold hers, and self-consciously, but deliberately, she returned the kiss. He was close enough that she could see his smile as he turned back toward the chutes. Trying not to look around her, Megan waited for the blood in her cheeks to subside. She supposed some women liked this kind of public recognition, but for her it was rather painful, especially since she knew he meant nothing special by it. He was just feeling high because he'd made a good ride. And he liked to share his triumph.

Megan watched for some time, even cheering as she watched Laina compete in the barrel race and feeling sorry when her time wasn't good enough. It was a curious thing, she supposed, that she did not actually dislike Laina. But after all, the barrel racer was really quite a nice person. She could hardly be blamed for loving Bart. Didn't Megan herself love him?

By the time the team roping came around, Megan was hot and tired. She was used to the Montana sun—her skin had already turned the color of buckwheat honey—but she was also used to the openness of the prairie. Even her few weeks' absence from crowded city life had changed her, she thought. She had grown to value the prairie's space and silence.

The beefy man on her right was sweating profusely now, occasionally mopping his face with the red bandanna around his neck. To her left sat several young boys, whose strident comments made her want to wince. If only these were the old days, she thought. If she were a pioneer wife. Bart's wife. And they could build a sod house on the great rolling land. How happily she could have lived there, with Bart as her man. But such things were not to be.

Megan sighed. Sweat was running down the valley between her breasts, her shirt was stuck damply to her back, and her jeans felt as if she'd gone swimming in them. She ran a hand under the heavy fall of hair that covered her neck. It was just too hot. Not a breeze stirring.

"The next event," said the announcer, "will be team roping. It takes skilled riders to coordinate their movements in this event, ladies and gentlemen. Skilled riders and skilled horses. The cowboy's horse is his best piece of equipment, and these horses are finely trained." He paused. "And here comes team number one. Look at those boys go."

The first rider missed his throw, and that team had no time. The second team fared only somewhat better, the first rider succeeding in lassoing the calf's head, but the second missing his try for the back legs.

Then the announcer's voice brought Megan's tired

form erect. "Team number three, Ed Arnett and Bart Dutton."

Much as she wanted to look only at Bart, Megan forced herself to watch the horse's right front leg. But she could not see that Dixie favored it in any way at all. Her stride seemed even and sure, and when Bart laid his loop skillfully over the calf's head and took two dallies around the saddle horn, she turned smoothly to pull the rope taut and face the calf. Their time was quite good, Megan thought, but of course there were still more teams to compete.

As the riders wheeled their horses to leave the arena, Bart's eyes searched her out again. And again Megan colored. But this time he didn't blow her a kiss. He just removed his hat and bowed toward her gravely.

A few minutes later a small boy approached Megan. "Lady? Are you a vet?"

Megan nodded, surprise in her eyes. "Yes, why?"

"There's a cowboy down in the stable area. He sent me up to get you." The youngster grinned. "He said you had red hair. And freckles like me."

Megan returned the grin. "Was he big, with black hair and blue eyes?"

"Yup." The boy turned. "He told me to show you how to get there." His grin widened. "He give me a dollar. Gonna give me another when I deliver you."

"Then I'd better come along, hadn't I?" she said, feeling suddenly more cheerful, and she rose and made her way past the beefy man and followed the boy down between the bleachers.

Five minutes later he walked her triumphantly up to Bart. "Here she is, mister. She is the right one, ain't she?"

Bart's grin was slow in coming, but finally he

nodded. "You got good eyes, boy. She's the one, all right. Here." He gave the boy two more bills.

"Gee, mister, thanks." The boy gave Megan a wicked grin. "Charge him high, doc. He looks like a big spender."

Megan laughed. There was not much else to do. She could hardly bring herself to look up into Bart's eyes. His words were still echoing in her ears. "She's the one, all right." Of course he only meant that the boy had concluded his errand, but oh, her heart cried, if only he had meant something else.

"I watched Dixie," she said, keeping her gaze on the plaid shirt that was level with her eyes. "I can't see anything wrong with her. Are you sure she was favoring it?"

"Megan. Look at me."

She could not resist the command, slowly raising her eyes to his.

"Are you sure Dixie was favoring her leg?" she repeated, knowing that she was babbling nervously, but unable to stop herself. "I don't know why you went to all the trouble and expense to fly me down here. The horse doesn't—"

Bart moved closer with every word she said until there was barely an inch between them. "Woman, be quiet," he commanded. But it was his tone rather than the words that stopped her, stopped her and made her heart pound.

"I thought you were a pretty smart female," he said. "But today you seem terrible dense."

"I don't understand," Megan began. Her breath was coming fast now. He was so close that her body yearned to touch him. Just to span those few inches that separated them from each other. To lean against his hard-muscled chest. She would have backed away, evaded him, but her back was against a wooden stall, and while she tried to decide which way to move, he took another step closer and settled one hand on either side of her shoulders, effectively pinning her there.

"Maybe," he said, his eyes glinting, "maybe you'll understand this." And, his hands sliding down to grip her waist, he lifted her bodily to meet his kiss. There was no way she could refuse him, no way to keep her body from responding to his. For this was what she wanted. She wanted it with every cell in her body. For a moment she was conscious of the warm horsy smell of the stables, the chomping of Dixie's jaws in the stall behind her. Then everything around her faded.

Nothing mattered but the warm embrace of his arms, pinning her body against his, her breasts crushed against his chest, his mouth heavy on hers. She tasted dust and salt on his lips before her body took over completely and she forgot everything except the rising desire to join herself with him, to belong to him.

It was a long kiss, long and thorough, and when he released her mouth, he let her body slide slowly down the front of his until her boots reached the floor. She was trembling with her need of him, words of love quivering in her heart. Her hands moved on the back of his shirt, feeling the hard muscles beneath the damp shirt. If they were alone at his moment, she knew that she would be unable to refuse him anything.

But they were not alone. Coming in she had seen several cowboys attending to their horses, and now that Bart was not blocking all her senses with his kisses she could hear others talking.

Against her cheek she felt the beating of his heart and knew its pace was fast, like hers. Bart's hand left her waist to reach up gently and tuck a wisp of hair behind her ear. "Now that that's settled, maybe I can get back to rodeoing. I'll see you at the room later." His eyes surveyed her critically. "You're looking kind of peaked. Maybe you'd better go lie down for a while. I've got a big evening planned."

"But Bart—"

What was "settled"? she wanted to ask. But he grinned and gave her a smart slap on the behind. "Run along, sugar. I got work to do."

He lifted her by the waist, setting her easily to one side. Unlatching the gate, he led Dixie out. "See you later," he said, his voice a caress.

"Okay." Megan hardly knew what she was saying. What did he mean by "settled"? she asked herself as she made her way back toward the motel, anxious for a cool shower and a nap in the air-conditioned room. "Settled." The word echoed and reechoed in her head. It would mean so much, she thought, her heart thudding. It could mean a future together. Or—her spirits fell quicker than a bucked-off rider—it could mean only that he wasn't mad at her anymore, that he meant to give her the night they had missed in Billings.

That must be what he meant, she told herself, hardly daring to think of the other alternative. But now she had to consider her choices. Was she willing to take this evening, to let it stand alone and not expect more? She was not sure. But if she took this evening, reached out and took what she wanted, as Bart had said, wasn't there the possibility that it could grow into something better, something with a future?

She reached the motel, almost in a daze, to find Laina Darwood standing outside the elevator.

"Hi, Megan." Laina's defeat in the barrel riding didn't seem to have affected her natural good spirits. "Been watching the action?"

Megan nodded. "Yes, but I'm afraid the heat's gotten to me."

"It can do that. Well, you'll enjoy the air conditioning in here." She smiled.

"I'm glad you got to see Bart in action," Laina continued. "We've been on the circuit together for years. It's a great life."

Megan could not agree with this, but she kept silent. She felt too good to argue with anyone.

The elevator stopped. "See you," Laina said. "Your room has a great view," she continued. "Enjoy it." This time there was something different, almost smug, in her smile, something that prickled at Megan's nerves.

The door closed and the elevator continued to the next floor. It had opened and Megan was walking out before the import of the words finally struck her. Laina knew about the view because *she* had been in the room. She had been there with Bart! That had to be it.

Probably they shared a room as they traveled the circuit, Megan thought. Laina must have realized why Bart had asked his vet up here.

Now Megan was confused. Didn't Laina mind if Bart slept with someone else? But maybe she didn't. Megan had heard of these new relationships in which people didn't expect faithfulness of their partners. She could not understand them, but she knew they existed.

For a moment Megan considered staying and taking what she could get. But as she shut the door to the room behind her, she knew she could not do it.

She might have considered staying on and having this night, even though it might only be for once, might have considered it if she could have *hoped* for more. For no matter what she had told herself, Bart's words had made her hope.

But now, now it was different. She had to face the fact that Bart belonged to Laina. Whatever he felt for his "lady vet" had nothing to do with love. He just wanted her for fun and games.

And she knew now with a driving certainty that she

could not go that route. Already her heart and mind were full of Bart. And she could think of nothing worse than spending her life being in love with another woman's husband. No, the best thing to do was to get out. Go back to the ranch and make arrangements to go elsewhere. She could be gone before Bart returned from the circuit. That had to be the thing to do.

Chapter Twelve

An hour later Megan was staring dully out the window of a bus headed for Miles City. She had thought about hiring a car, but she had to think about money. She didn't have a great deal, and she would have to be careful with it. So she had chosen the bus.

If it had had air conditioning, it had long ago ceased functioning, and the air coming through the opened window was hot and sticky. Megan sighed. She had not stopped for a shower before leaving, just grabbed her things and hurried out. Now she felt as though she'd gone swimming in her clothes. She ran a hand under the hair that lay sweltering against her neck and shifted it so that air could circulate there. What she wouldn't give for a nice cool room, she thought, the tears stinging her eyelids.

She was not going to cry. She was quite determined about that. Tears were useless in this situation. After all, it was not the first time a woman had loved and not had her love returned. She would survive it. It might

128

be difficult for her, since this was the first time that she had ever felt this way about a man.

Megan smiled ruefully. Her love had always been horses. Perhaps she would have been wiser to stick to them! They were much easier to understand than men.

She let her thoughts go to the great stallion, Diablo. She would miss him terribly, but it seemed clear that she had to leave the Rocking D. And she would have to do it when Bart wasn't around. Otherwise she might be unable to make the break.

But thinking of Bart was too painful. She would think of the great stallion instead. Surely before she left there would be time for one ride across the prairie, one ride to remember. She closed her eyes and let her head fall back against the seat.

The stopping of the bus some time later woke Megan from a doze. The flashing lights of a police cruiser reflected off the bus windows as the driver opened the door.

"Looking for a Dr. Megan Ryan," said the officer. "An emergency."

Megan came suddenly, violently awake. Bart! "Here," she cried. "I'm Dr. Ryan."

The officer motioned her forward, his face impassive. "We'll have to ask you to come with us," he said. "You're needed at the rodeo in Browning."

Megan's knees felt like rubber as she grabbed her bag and made her way forward. "What is it?" she asked. "What's happened?"

The officer shook his head. "We have no information on that. Just instructions to return you to Browning. Have you got luggage?"

"Yes, yes. One suitcase." Megan tried to calm herself. What could have happened? Had Bart been hurt? Or Dixie? Her hands went clammy as her mind presented her with the most horrifying pictures. Bart being trampled. Bart in a hospital bed. Bart with a sheet over his crumpled body, a sheet that covered his face.

Hardly knowing what she did, she allowed the policeman to guide her to the cruiser and help her inside. The ride back to Browning seemed to take days. Megan's frantic mind raced in circles as she tried to make sense out of what was happening.

It was almost dark when the car finally pulled into the motel parking lot. Megan looked around her. "What are we doing here?" she asked.

The officer shrugged. "Our orders said deliver you here. That's all we know. Can you make it to your room all right? They said someone would be there to fill you in."

She nodded. "Of course." She was helped out of the car and handed her suitcase, then the cruiser drove off. On trembling legs Megan hurried into the motel. The elevator seemed to take forever, and her quivering hand kept missing the keyhole. Finally she got the door open and burst into the room, looking around wildly for some kind of note.

The suitcase fell from her numbed fingers as she spied the recumbent figure on the bed. He got slowly to his feet and crossed the room to close the door. When he turned, she had regained some of her senses. He was all right. It had to be his prized roping horse. "What happened?" she asked. "What's wrong with Dixie?"

His voice was even, his expression mild. "Nothing."

The word hit her like a slap. He had dragged her all the way back here, scared her half to death, and nothing was wrong! Her fatigue vanished to be replaced by a wave of white hot anger.

"How dare you do this to me?" she cried, her fingers

curling into fists. "Letting me think you were hurt? Maybe dead?"

Bart's mild expression disappeared. "You should talk! How could you do that to me? Running out on me just when I thought everything was settled."

"Settled?" Megan's Irish temper was flaming now. "Things are settled, all right. Laina may not mind being put out so you can share this room with me, but I mind. How dare you treat me like that?"

Bart's face darkened and his voice took on new timbre in his fury. "What the hell are you. talking about?" he demanded.

"I saw Laina earlier. On the elevator." Megan hung on to her anger. It was her only defense against him. "She told me how you shared this room."

"She *what?*"

Megan took a step backward, unconsciously retreating from his baffled rage.

"She—" Megan tried to remember Laina's exact words. "She implied that the two of you shared this room." There was nowhere to retreat to now; the wall was at her back.

"Implied," he said sarcastically. "What the hell does that mean? What did she *say?* Exactly what did she say? Come on, give me the exact words."

Megan's fatigue came rolling back in great waves that almost knocked her legs from under her. "I—I can't remember exactly. Wait! She told me to enjoy the view."

Bart's fingers clenched into fists as he fought his own temper. "So you immediately jumped to the wrong conclusion."

"I—she made it very clear to me." Megan's tongue stumbled over the words as she fought the conflicting waves of feeling. Part of her was still raging mad, wanting to scream and yell at him. But another part was exhausted and so relieved to see him alive that she wanted to throw herself into his arms and sob for joy. She wanted to believe him, she thought. She wanted it so much. For if she believed him, she might not have to leave the Rocking D.

"What seems clear to me," he said in tones of disgust, "is that you're determined to think the worst of me." He frowned even more, his heavy black eyebrows almost meeting. "From the first minute you set eyes on me in Miles City, you made up your mind."

"That isn't true!" Megan shouted. "I just don't— that is—"

"I know," he said sharply. "You don't mess around with strangers you meet on the street. I can accept that. But I'm not exactly a stranger now. Am I, Megan?" His eyes clouded and grew warm, and she felt the blood rushing to her cheeks.

"No, but—"

"You're angry," he said harshly, "because I didn't let you run out on me. Well, I'm angry, too. I'm tired of this song and dance you've been giving me. One day hot, next day cold. I'm tired of waiting." He let his eyes slide over her. It was almost as though his hands had touched her. Her body quivered with desire for him. It hit her so strongly that she felt her breasts tingle under the damp shirt. For a moment she stared into those smoldering eyes.

Then with a muttered curse he crossed the space that separated them and yanked her against him. If she had wanted to protest, there would have been no time. One second she felt her breasts pressing against his chest, his thighs hard against hers, and the next his mouth had found hers.

It was a short kiss—angry, rather savage, but it made her blood race and her pulse quicken, and she could not stop herself from responding to it. Then, just as abruptly as he had grabbed her, he released her and stood glaring down at her. "Goddamn it, woman! You're driving me crazy. Now you listen to me. And listen good. That is it. I want you. And I'm no boy; I know damn well you want me." He licked his lips. "But I'm not doing any more begging. See that door?" He pointed to a door that obviously led to the next room.

Dumbly, Megan nodded.

"Well, I'm going through that door. I'm going to take a shower and relax. If you want me, you open that door and you come to me. Now, is that clear?" His eyes bored into hers.

"Yes." She could not very well deny wanting him, not after that night in Billings and this last kiss. She decided to forget all the old rules and be honest with him. "Of course I want you," she began. "But Laina—"

He threw up his hands in disgust. "Damn it, woman! Laina has nothing to do with you and me. Nothing at all."

"But—"

"No! I don't want to talk about it anymore." He crossed the room to the connecting door. "You know where to find me, Megan. The rest is up to you." And he opened the door and stepped through, closing it firmly behind him.

For a long moment Megan remained standing there, staring at the door. Laina had nothing to do with them, he said. Now what did he mean by that?

Suddenly she was conscious of her disheveled condition. She was hot and sticky, her hair a tangled mess. The first thing to do was to take a shower. She stripped off her dirty clothes and headed for the bathroom.

The water was deliciously cool, and she washed her hair, letting the water cascade over her in great cleansing streams. She tried to concentrate on it, to obliterate everything else from her mind, but she was not successful. He wanted her, he said. And he knew she wanted him. Her nipples grew erect at the thought of his touch. How much she yearned for the feel of his body against her own. Even the cool water could not stop the flaming of her cheeks at the recollection of the pleasure they had shared in Billings. Of course she wanted him. It was only Laina who stood between them. And he had said Laina had nothing to do with them. Perhaps she really didn't care what he did.

Megan's thoughts whirled chaotically as she toweled herself and her hair. No man had ever laid things so clearly on the line before. Certainly none had ever asked her to come to him like that. But no man had ever meant to her what Bart did.

She finished drying and paused to look at herself in the mirror. What she saw startled her. Her face was flushed with desire, her eyes shining, her breasts swollen. How she wanted him.

Be sensible, she told herself. He wants you. You want him. He knows it. Why not behave as a man would? Reach for what you want. That's what he would do.

The standard objections rose to Megan's mind, but she shook her head. She was tired of fighting her love for him, tired of thinking about the future. Tonight she was going to take what she wanted. Let tomorrow take care of itself for a change. If this made a difference in their employer-employee relationship so that she could no longer work at the Rocking D, what would she have lost? She had already decided that she couldn't stay on there.

She had never been one for one-night stands, but then this would be their second night. And if he had wanted her after the first time, perhaps he would want her after this time. And though it was not love, wanting could be a prelude to it.

She ran the brush once more through her hair and slid into her robe. For once in her life she was going to do what she wanted to do, and do it without worrying about the future. She crossed the room and opened the connecting door.

He was lying flat on his back on the bed, his powerful body naked in the dim light. Megan paused, one hand still on the doorknob. He turned his head, alerted by the opening of the door, and looked at her. His eyes held invitation, but he did not move, waiting for her to decide, to move into the room or to withdraw. She took a deep breath and stepped in, closing the door behind her.

"Hello," he said, his eyes caressing her so that her silk robe seemed suddenly transparent. "I'm glad you came."

"I—" Megan didn't know what to say.

"Come here," he invited, stretching out one well-muscled arm. Absently she noted how brown it was. The top half of his body was all deep brown, the bottom half much paler. She moved toward him, her bare feet soundless on the carpet.

He patted the bed beside him. "Sit down."

Megan sat. She tried to keep her eyes on his face, away from the powerful body so close to her. But her fingers ached to touch him, to feel his flesh under her hands.

Almost as though he could read her mind, he smiled and reached up to take one of her hands. He kissed the palm. "You can touch," he said, laying it gently on his flat stomach. "I don't break."

"I—" Again Megan felt at a loss for words.

"You act like you've never done this before," he said, his voice teasing.

"I haven't, not really." She stroked the warm flesh under her fingers. "I've been busy," she said. "Going to school and all. I—haven't had many boyfriends."

"You're doing just great," he said with a lazy smile, slipping a hand inside her robe where it came to rest on her trembling thigh.

"You're not cold, are you?" he asked.

Megan shook her head. "No."

"Then let's take this thing off." His fingers moved to untie it as he spoke, and he slipped it down over her shoulders, revealing her breasts, gleaming in the dim light.

"Beautiful," he said reverently. "Just beautiful." And he raised himself on one elbow and took a rosy nipple in his mouth.

A surge of pure joy raced through Megan, and she moaned softly. His hands on her elbows held her erect; otherwise she would have fallen, so intense was the pleasure his act gave her. He released that nipple only to repeat the process with the other. His hands stripped the robe from her. It fell unheeded to the floor as he pulled her down beside him. Her head fit comfortably against his shoulder, her breasts pressing against his chest. A deep sigh of contentment welled out of her. This was where she belonged, here, next to the man she loved.

He ran one hand lightly up her bare arm to her throat, tracing the contours of her ear. Megan shivered and pushed closer against him, her breasts sensitive to the crisp curling hair of his chest. He picked up a strand of her hair and drew it across her earlobe, then up her throat and cheek to her forehead. "I love your hair," he whispered. "So soft." He drew a strand across his own chin. "Like silk."

Megan's fingers moved up to touch his unruly black hair, moved down to caress his freshly shaven cheek.

With one finger she traced the warm curve of his lips, jumped startled when his tongue flicked out to touch it as it passed. "You scared me," she whispered.

He breath was warm on her forehead. "Now or before?" he asked.

She buried her face in his neck. "Both," she murmured.

"No need to be scared," he said, his hands moving up her back, caressing the soft skin, then settling on the sensitive nape of her neck. Tremors of desire raced through her.

"Oh, Megan," he groaned. "Why did you keep me off for so long?"

"I—" She thought about telling him, but to bring Laina into this would destroy it. She didn't want to think of Laina; she wanted to think only of the two of them. "It doesn't matter now," she replied softly.

She moved her hand down to his chest, playing with the dark hair that curled there, feeling the warm flesh under her fingers. His hand curled around hers, carrying it farther down his body. Megan followed his lead, caressing his flat stomach and down farther to his manhood.

"Mmmmm," he said. "Feels good."

His fingers reached out to her left breast, and she pressed closer against his side as he drew slow, tantalizing circles around her nipple. Her body moved against his, and her breath began to quicken.

He raised his head so he could reach her breast with his mouth, leaving little wet kisses over its white roundness until finally he took the erect nipple into his mouth. Megan's body thrust upward of its own accord.

He shifted her to her back and got to his knees beside her. Now the whole of her body lay open to his exploring hands. He traced every curve of it, slowly, reverently, as though seeing it for the first time.

Her body yearned toward him, wanting to feel the whole of him against her needy flesh, but he took his time, exploring every inch of her with hands and mouth. He left a trail of kisses from the valley between her breasts, down across the smooth flatness of her belly, to the mound of auburn hair and her most secret place.

She moved beneath his questing hands, accepting his most intimate caresses with a rising joy. He was there, wanting her, and soon, soon now, he would take her, joining his hard masculine flesh to her soft feminine form. She wanted that moment, wanted it terribly, yet she also wanted to postpone it, to experience a little longer the near-ecstasy to which he had brought her.

Whatever part of him was within reach, her searching hands found and caressed. She felt the smoothness of his back, the crisp texture of the hair on his legs. The muscles of his arms moved under her fingers, and she was vaguely conscious of the strength that lay there. These were the arms that kept him on the back of a bucking bronc, but they had only gentleness for her. There was none of the rage she had felt in him before, only a tenderness and need.

Finally he eased himself down on top of her. "God, Megan," he cried hoarsely. "I can't wait any longer. I need you."

She opened herself to receive him, sighing with pleasure as he entered and wrapping her arms around him. "I need—you, too," she whispered, her fingers digging into his shoulders as he thrust into her. Waves of pleasure spread outward from her center. She was nothing but feeling. Everything was obliterated from her mind except their two bodies, moving in unison, in the oldest dance in time.

Closer and closer came the final moment. They were both gasping for breath. His arms were under her shoulders, clasping her to him. Hers were around him, holding him as close as she could. She heard his breathing change, felt him surging inside her, and at that same moment came her own release. So intense was it that she clung to him, quivering with the aftershock, planting little kisses along the curve of his shoulder.

"You shouldn't have made me wait so long," he murmured when he regained his breath. "Weeks and weeks of wanting you. From the first day I saw you on the street," he continued. "I was attracted to you then. But I suppose you knew that." He rolled slowly over, pulling her after him to lie against his side.

When she didn't answer, he ran a hand down her side. "When did you know?" he asked.

Megan was still floating in a warm sea of contentment. "I don't know. For sure after we delivered the foal. Before that . . ." She smiled. "You don't need to be told that you're an attractive man."

He chuckled and wrapped his other arm around her. "You didn't think so that day on the street."

"It's different for women," she said. "At least, for me. When I see an attractive man, I don't make a play for him."

"You don't have to," he said. "If he's got eyes, he'll make one for you."

He didn't see the point, Megan knew, but she could not bring herself to go on. If she told him that she didn't go to bed with strangers, he would think she was some kind of prude. Nor would he have believed her if she'd told him how Sunrise's birth had altered her feelings about him. Men didn't let things like that interfere with what they wanted.

"So, it was the filly's birth that did it," he mused, his hand caressing her absently. "Come to think of it, that sort of changed my thinking about you, too. You've got guts, Megan my love. Guts and spunk."

She hardly heard the compliment for the endearment. "Megan my love." How sweet the words sounded.

"Thank you, sir," she replied playfully. "I'm glad my talents are appreciated."

"Oh, they are. They are indeed," he continued, his face breaking into a grin.

Megan buried her face in his neck, embarrassed by what she saw in his eyes.

"You're a beautiful woman, love," he said softly. "Just as beautiful as I remember you from that night in Billings. That was a good night."

"Yes," Megan agreed softly. "But tonight was better."

"It was, wasn't it?" He smiled and hugged her closer for a moment. "I think it has something to do with that old saying 'Practice makes perfect.'" His fingers stroked her smooth belly. "I've a feeling we're going to get plenty of that. Now that you're not running anymore. You're not, are you?"

"No, Bart, I'm not running." As she repeated the words, she smiled. There was no need to run now. He spoke as though they had a future. What that future entailed, she did not know. But at this moment she didn't want to ask. She felt safe now, here in his arms. This was where she wanted to be. Beyond that she could not and would not think.

Chapter Thirteen

Megan was wakened the next morning by a warm hand on her breast. She opened her eyes slowly, vaguely aware of a sense of great well-being, and then, as the possessive hand registered in her head, she realized where she was. She was lying spoon-fashion on her side and Bart was behind her, her curves fitting against him perfectly. He had one arm around her and was playing with her breast, teasing the nipple into a rosy peak. She felt desire rising up in her again.

"Good morning, Megan my love." He made it sound like one word, a word of deep endearment. "And how are you this morning?" he asked, his lips against her ear.

She sighed and snuggled back against him. "I think perhaps I've been dreaming," she replied sleepily. "Dreaming the most wonderful dreams."

He moved far enough to shift her onto her back. She looked up at his face, his eyes still heavy with sleep. His hair was all tousled and his chin showed the beginning of a beard, but his grin was wide. "Maybe we were both in the same dream," he said softly, kissing her bare shoulder. "Mine was wonderful, too."

She put her arms around his neck and pulled him close, kissing him fiercely.

"Easy, woman," he said when she released him. "Got to give a man time to get his bones working." As he shifted his weight, she saw a spasm of pain cross his face.

"Bart, what is it?"

His grin came back and he kissed her briefly on the nose. "What a worrywart you are. Gonna have to get used to this if you're gonna be a bronc rider's woman."

The words warmed her to a lovely glow, but she was still concerned. "Get used to what?" she said, her eyes anxious.

"To my moaning and groaning in the mornings," he said, kissing her forehead. "When a man's got as many patched-up places as I do, well, it takes him a little longer to get started in the morning. Places like that are apt to stiffen on a man."

"Oh, Bart, why don't you get out of this business? Your bucking stock is doing well. Settle down and live a normal life."

He shook his head. "Like I told you before, I've thought about it. But the ranch is always needing something. And rodeo prize money's not to be sneezed at. To say nothing of being a champion."

"I know. It's just—" She stopped suddenly, aware that she was taking too much for granted. Being Bart's woman didn't mean she could tell him what to do.

"Just what?" he asked, bending to nuzzle her ear. *Just that I love you*, she wanted to say, but instead she made her voice light. "We can't 'practice' if you get yourself laid up."

His laugh rang out, warm and full. "Don't you worry about that, Megan my love. I'll be very careful. The

Rocking D's going to see a lot of its boss this season, and so are you."

"When is the season over?" Megan asked.

"Never, really. But it begins officially in January and ends in December."

"So long." So many opportunities to be hurt. "But you don't have to work the entire season."

"Don't *have* to," he said. "But championship points are based on prize money, you know. So it pays to keep hopping. In more ways than one. Speaking of which . . ." He eased himself to a sitting position on the side of the bed. "I'd better get my tail moving."

Turning to look at her, he caught the disappointment on her face before she could hide it, and he laughed. "C'mon, honey. Wash my back for me." His grin was brazen. "Then I'll do something nice for you."

As she followed him into the small bathroom, Megan wondered at how swiftly things could change. Yesterday she had been the most miserable woman in the world. And today? Today she was floating on air.

She pinned her hair high on top of her head while Bart adjusted the water. "Nice and hot," he said, running a hand over her bottom. "Hope it doesn't dry out that pretty skin."

She copied the caress on his bottom and grinned. "Doesn't seem to have hurt yours any."

He lunged for her playfully, but she evaded him, knowing as she did so that in the small bathroom he could have cornered her easily. He stepped into the shower and gestured to her. "Come on, woman. Do your duty."

Joining him there, she took the soap he offered her. "Now that you're here," he said, grinning, "you might as well do the whole job. But don't take too long. I got a job I intend doing myself. And I want time to do it right." His caressing fingers made it quite clear what he intended to do.

Megan smiled to herself as she began to soap the powerful body before her. She had to reach up to do his shoulders, and he steadied her, wet hands on her slim waist. "Better hurry, woman," he threatened. "Or I'll have you right here on the shower floor."

Megan laughed. "We wouldn't fit. Besides, wouldn't that be hard on your bones?"

He shrugged. "The hot water's loosened them up good."

She had reached his chest now, and she soaped it thoroughly, concentrating on the pleasure she felt from touching him. Her hands dropped lower still, soaping and caressing. She washed his lean hard stomach. He had the body of an athlete, she thought as he turned, presenting her his back. She soaped it, too, reaching up to the muscular shoulders, running a soapy hand down his spine.

She was ready to move farther down, to the firm rounded buttocks, when he turned again. "My turn," he said, taking the soap from her fingers.

And, suiting his actions to his words, he began to soap her. It was incredibly sensuous; the warm water, the slippery suds, and Bart's caressing fingers. He stood her out of reach of the shower's spray and covered her from hips to shoulders with a froth of soap bubbles.

"There," he exclaimed. "That's the only kind of covering you need."

Looking down, Megan saw that the suds concealed practically nothing. Her nipples were thrust out toward him and her whole body tingled from the touch of his hands.

Those same hands moved down, gently soaping the most secret of her places, and her knees went weak. She laid her head against his wet shoulder as he bent before her, and she was not sure she could remain standing for long.

Just when she thought her legs were going to give way for sure, he straightened and pushed her under the cleansing spray. Turning her lightly in place, he ran his hands over her in long smooth strokes.

She stepped out of the spray and reached for the soap, her hands moving quickly to his most private parts.

Suddenly he gave a great groan and grabbed her by the waist. "That does it," he cried. "Can't wait."

And he picked her bodily off her feet and yanked back the curtain.

"Bart! The water!"

"Always causing problems," he said, his free hand reaching for the faucet. "Now you just be quiet. I'm running this show."

"Yes, sir." Megan wrapped her arms around his neck, thankful that her less than a hundred pounds made her relatively easy to carry.

He took her directly to the bed and dumped her there. "I'll teach you to get me riled up," he said, frowning in mock severity. "Next time you'll know better."

A giggle spilled from Megan's lips. "You look funny."

"Do I now?" he growled. "And how do you suppose you look? All wet and shiny like that?"

He groaned again and threw himself on her. "Woman! You're enough to drive a man out of his mind!"

And then he was in her and she was ready, ready and eager for the thrust of his hard body against her own. It was over soon, far too soon, she thought, as the ecstasy overcame her. For she knew that there would be no pleasant lingering in the bed this morning;

no additional reachings for her as he had reached in the night just passed.

He did not leave her immediately, though, and she clung to him, impressing the feel of his body on her memory. Finally he spoke, his tone full of regret. "Sorry, honey. I'd much rather stay here with you, but the rodeo's waiting."

She kissed his shoulder. "I know, Bart. The rodeo is always first." She was herself surprised by the slight touch of bitterness in her voice, but he did not pick up on it so perhaps he didn't catch it.

He raised himself on his elbows and looked down at her. "You're enough to make a man forget his name, let alone his job." He kissed the tip of her nose, then both eyelids. "Do me a favor, honey." He waited for her nod. "When I get up, pull the covers up around your neck and stay put till I leave. I have to move on this afternoon, quick as the winners are named. Otherwise I won't make the next one on time."

She fought to keep her expression calm. Already he was leaving her.

"You do understand, don't you, Megan?"

She forced herself to answer him then. "I understand."

"Good. I'll get back to see you whenever I can. A week, maybe two, between times. Okay?"

"Okay," she said. Once every week or two. To see the man she loved, to lie next to him. But it was better than nothing, she told herself. Far better than nothing. She touched his cheek tenderly. "I'll be there. Waiting."

"Good." He bent his head again and kissed her soundly, so soundly that she forgot everything except her longing for him.

He lifted himself from her abruptly, turning his back

on her. "Maybe you'd better cover your head, too, or else I'll never get out of here."

She reached obediently for the covers and pulled them up around her neck. She could not bring herself to cover her head. Every sight of him was precious; she did not want to miss one second of seeing him. She watched him cross the room, his lean body moving with a swift grace that belied his talk about old aching bones.

He disappeared from her sight long enough to take a quick shower, then he was back in the room, toweling his wet hair. His eyes sought her out, and he grinned at the sight of the covers up around her neck. "That's my girl."

She stuck a hand out and made as though to uncover herself. "Woman," she reminded him.

His grin grew wider. "Woman," he acknowledged. "My woman."

Megan felt the tears rising and swallowed quickly. How much those words meant. But she could not let him see her cry.

Her silence made him eye her questioningly. "Aren't you?" he said, those blue eyes boring into hers.

She forced herself to smile. "Yes, Bart. I am."

"Good." He shrugged into a shirt and pulled on his jeans, then settled onto the side of the bed to tug on his socks.

Megan clenched her hands into fists to keep from reaching out to touch him. He was so close. Yet she wanted to respect his wishes. And she knew the rodeo was important to him. She settled for voicing her thoughts—in a way. "I wish I could help you on with your boots."

"Nothing doing," he said with mock ferocity. "You move those covers and I'm a goner." He gave her a quick pat through the blanket. Then he was on his feet,

knotting a bandanna around his neck. "There'll be a
car here to pick you up at nine-thirty. Take you out to
the plane. And Pete'll be waiting at the other end.
Take good care of the place for me, especially Sunrise."

She held her breath. Don't let him warn her away
from the stallion, she prayed. For if he elicited a
promise from her now . . .

He put the change off the dresser into his pocket
and picked up his Stetson. She held herself still,
wanting to throw back the covers and run into his
arms. He moved up to the head of the bed. "Don't
move," he warned. "Don't touch me."

He bent and put one hand on either side of her
head. "One more kiss. To keep me till I get home."
His lips touched hers briefly, then he straightened.
"Got to run, love. Don't forget. One week. Maybe
two."

"I won't forget, Bart." His hand was on the
doorknob. "Bart . . ." She swallowed over the lump in
her throat. "Please be careful."

His eyes grew sober. "Woman, you worry too much.
Behave yourself, now." And he blew her a kiss as he
had in the arena. "See you soon."

The door shut firmly. For several moments Megan
lay there, trying to retain the sight and feel of him. The
tears were dangerously close, but she blinked them
back. One or two weeks, he had said. She would make
that time pass quickly, she told herself as she pushed
back the covers and got to her feet.

She would spend the time with Diablo. A frown
creased her forehead. When Bart was at home, she
would not be able to see the stallion. He was wrong
about the horse; she was sure of that. But she could
not tell him so. Not now, at least.

*   *   *

It was after noon when Megan climbed into the car where Pete waited. "Hi there, lass." His gray eyes surveyed her shrewdly. "Have a good trip?"

Megan wondered if her face would give her away, but she kept her voice even. "Yes, Pete. The rodeo was very exciting. I've never seen one live before."

"Uh huh." His grin reflected his amusement. "I can see it was exciting. Made your cheeks rosy and your eyes sparkle."

"How's Arabica?" she asked. "And Sunrise?"

"Same as always," he replied. "Doing fine. Filly's growing like a bad weed."

"Do you think she'll make a good bucker?" she asked, hoping to keep him from asking any more questions.

"Too early to tell," Pete said. "Lucky thing that good buckers ain't spoiled by tender loving care. Or you'd ruin all ours."

Megan grinned. "Can't help it, Pete. You know I love horses."

"Yeah, I know." He looked as though he might add something more.

But Megan did not wait. "It seemed funny to me when I first found out that bucking horses don't hate people."

"Except Diablo," Pete pointed out.

"Diablo doesn't hate people," Megan reiterated, her defense of the stallion automatic.

"Bart thinks so," Pete said, his voice sober. "And if you don't stay away from that horse, there's gonna be all kinds of trouble."

Megan's heart skipped a beat. "What do you mean?"

Pete's eyes left the road momentarily. "You might be able to fool Bart," he said. "He's away too much to see what you're doing. And the boys got work that keeps 'em busy. But I ain't so stupid. I know where you go when you're out on the range."

"Oh, Pete." She didn't try to deny it. "He's a wonderful horse, and I know he wouldn't hurt me."

"Maybe not," he agreed. "But that don't cut no ice with Bart. When he says stay away from something, he means it."

"I know, but . . ." She pleaded with her eyes. "You won't tell him, will you?"

" 'Course not." Pete's smile was grim. "Me, I don't want no trouble. I just don't like to see you get yourself hurt."

"I know, Pete." Megan gave him a warm smile.

Pete nodded. "You know, all right, but you ain't gonna listen."

"Oh, Pete, I can't. You know I can't. Diablo, he's—he's something special."

Pete shook his head. "Women. Don't pay no never mind to what you tell 'em. Always thinking they know best."

"Pete." She couldn't help laughing. "That's not true. You know it isn't. I don't claim *always* to be right. Just about horses."

Pete did not smile. "Being right ain't everything, you know. Sometimes being right costs more'n you want to pay."

Megan shook her head. This was not a thing she wanted to discuss any further. She loved Bart, and she thought Pete knew it. But that did not mean that she was willing to say she was wrong when she knew she was not. Bart was a good man; he loved horses, too. If she tamed Diablo, he would be able to accept that. He had to be.

She saw Pete's look as an hour later she swung up on the little mare and headed for the west range. But she couldn't help herself. She had to see the stallion,

had to be sure he was all right. She pushed the little
mare into a canter, keeping a careful eye out for the
telltale mounds of prairie-dog holes. Again she felt that
powerful pull toward the stallion, as though being with
him was like being with Bart.

After her drink in the creek, the mare moved automatically to the tree where she was usually hitched.
Megan looked around anxiously. Diablo must be
around somewhere. She had only missed being with
him one day. She slid down under a tree and rested her
chin in her hand.

She let her eyes drop shut and her thoughts drift
back to that morning, to the night before. Unconsciously she smiled. Bart's arms around her. Bart's
mouth on hers. Bart's body against hers. Her own body
warmed at the thought. One week. Two weeks at the
most, he had said. And he would be home. To see *her.*

She hugged herself, wrapping her arms around her
shoulders. *My woman,* Bart had said. She could hardly
believe it. Yet he had said it. And meant it. She was
sure of that.

A soft velvet nose pushed against her cheek, and
Megan's eyes flew open. "So there you are." She got to
her feet in one fluid motion and buried her face in his
satiny neck. "Did you miss me, boy? I missed you."

She pulled the great head around and rubbed her
cheek against the softness of his nose. The horse
whuffled and nudged her gently.

Megan laughed. "You greedy thing, you. You love
me for my sugar, not myself." She reached into her
pocket and got him a cube of sugar. He took it from
her palm, his teeth barely touching her skin as he lifted
it neatly.

She rubbed his ears affectionaly as he nudged her
again. "No more today," Megan said. "I've got to get
back now. Pete'll be having fits. Pete's a good guy. So's

Bart." She laughed. "Just because they're men doesn't mean they're no good. You're male yourself, you know. You just need to give them a chance." She rubbed again behind his ears. "But you will. Eventually. I'll get you to see the light." She laughed again as he nudged at her. "Them, too."

She ran a gentle hand up his shoulder and across his gleaming flank. "Oh, but you're a beauty," she crooned. "I want to ride you so much. Tomorrow," she promised him—and herself—as she moved back toward the mare. "I'll see you tomorrow. Maybe, maybe, you'll let me have a ride."

Chapter Fourteen

It was several days later before Megan felt she could think of spending much time with the stallion. A rash of small ailments seemed to occur among the horse herd; a suspected sprain here, a scratched fetlock there. Megan was rather sure that Pete was searching them out. But there was nothing she could say to him about it.

Finally, she felt that everything at the ranch was in order and that she could conceivably spend several hours away. She rose even earlier than usual, moving quietly in the early dawn, anxious to saddle Darling and get away before Pete got up and found something else for her to attend to.

She sighed as Darling moved out toward the west range. It went against the grain, her disobeying Bart's injunctions. And she knew that Pete's advice was well meant. But they were both wrong about the stallion. Megan felt that to the very bottom of her soul. Diablo was not a killer horse. He did not need to be "tamed"; he needed to be loved.

She pulled her jacket tighter. The early-morning air was chill. The prairie was silent, the only sound the plop of the mare's hooves and the rustle of the prairie grass as they passed. Occasionally she heard the clear call of a meadow lark or some other bird celebrating the new morning. As the sun rose higher the sky grew lighter. Megan smoothed the mare's neck and sighed. "Today's the day, Darling. Today I'm going to ride Diablo. At least I'm going to mount him." A quick smile lit her face. "I suppose Bart would think it served me right if he bucks me off. But I don't think he will."

She shifted a little in the saddle. "He knows me now. And I'm not a man."

Megan was not so naive that she didn't realize that mounting the stallion could be a very dangerous business. They were isolated out here on the prairie. If Diablo threw her—as he could if he bucked, for bareback she hadn't a chance of staying on—she could be very badly injured.

"But I've got to do it, Darling." The mare's ears turned back as she heard her name. "I've got to ride him. And then I've got to show Bart." She sighed again. "That will be the hard part. But he's not an unreasonable man. And surely if he loves me . . ."

The words hung in the air. He hadn't said he loved her. It had certainly *seemed* that he did. Megan's whole body went hot at the memories of their time together. It was still fresh in her mind: the way he had looked at her, the way he had caressed her, the way he had talked to her. *My woman.* He had said that. And he'd said he'd be home every week or two to see her. Surely that meant something.

The little mare ambled along, headed toward the west range. Megan's mind, however, was not there on the prairie. She missed Bart; she missed him more than she had thought it possible to miss a man. Alone at night in her room, she could not sleep for remembering the feel of his kisses. What wonderful things he could do to her with his mouth and his hands. She could see his hands in her mind's eye, large hands, browned by the sun, roughened by work and riding, but so tender, so knowing. How easily he had sought out all her secret places, bringing her pleasure such as she had never known existed.

Megan shifted on the saddle and the mare cocked an inquiring ear, but no command was forthcoming and she continued on her way, her rider oblivious to the sights around her. Three days, Megan thought, three whole days had passed since she'd been with Bart. For a moment she was racked with anxiety. What if he got hurt again?

In her mind she saw the network of scars on his chest, scars that even the mat of dark curly hair couldn't hide. Someday she would ask; she would lie beside him in the quiet afterward and trace them with an inquiring finger. And he would tell her how he got each one.

The one on his forehead she knew about already, of course. In fact, she had kissed it as she had kissed all the parts of him available to her. Her mind, like a videotape replaying, showed her his face—darkened by the sun, lined by years of exposure, not handsome, exactly, but so very attractive, especially when one met those bright-blue eyes and the flashing charming smile. That morning, that wonderful morning that she had wakened beside him, he'd been flushed with sleep, his hair, usually unruly, even more tousled. But somehow he had looked younger, less careworn.

Quite vividly her mind showed her Bart's body: the strong muscular arms that had embraced her with tenderness and passion; the dark, hair-covered chest that had felt so good against her naked breasts; the lean flat stomach that lay above his masculinity; his strong thighs and legs, also covered with fine black hair.

She could see him bending over to kiss her, see him walking away, his smooth hard-muscled back and rounded buttocks. Megan reached up to adjust her Stetson. Her breasts were swelling, she realized, her nipples pressing so hard against the lacy material of her bra that she could see their outline through her shirt.

Deep within her she felt the stirrings of desire, desire that plagued her every night since her return. How did the rodeo wives stand it, she thought, having their men gone so much of the time? If she and Bart were married, she would follow him—though watching him compete would be sheer agony. If only he would retire and settle down as Pete wanted.

Resolutely Megan pushed such thoughts away. It was too soon to think of marriage. She was Bart's woman, and that was enough for now. In a week and a half at the most he would be back to see her. To hold her and kiss her. To make love to her all night long. Maybe even in the morning. A long leisurely morning in bed. Again desire surged through her, desire so intense that she was almost embarrassed by it.

Until now she had not given much thought to love. Earning her degree had been a difficult and time-consuming task, especially since she had also worked part-time to pay her tuition. But now, now Bart seemed to be on her mind all the time. In the middle of the most mundane task she would see his face or think of something he had said and wanting him would be a tangible, physical ache in her insides.

The mare had reached the little grove of cottonwoods and stopped. Looking around her, Megan smiled. Darling had certainly made this trip on her own. She dismounted and gave the mare her regular drink before hitching her to the usual tree.

The stallion appeared before she was through. With nimble fingers Megan unbuckled the flap of the saddlebags and pulled out the bridle she carried there. There was never any problem slipping it on the stallion. He offered his neck to her expectantly, relishing the sugar cube he had learned would follow.

Megan smiled. "You're a greedy old thing," she said. "If I even run out of sugar, I suppose I'll lose your love."

The stallion whickered and rubbed his nose against her shoulder. Megan smiled. "All right, fellow. I believe you."

With the bridle on, she began to walk. The stallion followed patiently, as he had on previous days. He was docile and gentle, she told herself. He loved her.

But was that love strong enough? Strong enough to conquer his aversion to being ridden? Strong enough to conquer what by now must be an automatic response? Megan's heart thudded in her breast. She would never know if she did not put him to the test. And there would never be a better day than this one to do it in.

She walked him carefully toward a tree stump. Diablo was a big horse. She could not hope to mount him bareback without something to stand on. She smiled grimly. She was a good rider, but she was not a stuntwoman. No spectacular flying-through-the-air mounts for Megan Ryan.

She stopped the stallion beside the stump and turned to face him, pulling his head down toward hers. "Now listen, boy. This is important." She supposed people would think her crazy for talking to the horse like this, but somehow it helped. Besides, she had been talking to horses all her life, and it had almost always worked.

"It's important," she continued, "because I trust

you. I'm counting on your trust in me. There's not too much of me." She laughed nervously. "And the ground's going to be a long way down. Remember that, will you?" she pleaded, looking into the stallion's great dark eyes.

She wished she could take courage from those eyes, but as the moment of truth approached, she was growing more and more apprehensive. If she didn't get up on him soon, she would lose her nerve. And then she would despise herself. All her life she had had the courage of her convictions, acting in accord with what she believed. And she believed in Diablo.

She gathered the reins in her left hand and climbed up on the stump. He would have to stand still, she thought, or she would never make it. "Easy, boy," she crooned. "Easy now." She put both hands in his mane and swung her leg high. Seconds later she was astride the broad back. The stallion moved skittishly, her weight making him dance sideways. She held herself in readiness for that first kick. It wouldn't take any fancy sunfishing to unseat her. One simple kick would be more than sufficient to topple her onto the prairie.

But the stallion did not kick. He pranced a little, then turned his head around to stare at her from a curious eye. Megan relaxed, her relief bubbling over into laughter. If it were possible for a horse to look surprised, she would have said that of Diablo. He was surprised, but he still did not buck.

"So far, so good," muttered Megan, taking another deep breath. After all, she meant to ride the stallion, not just sit on him. She touched him gently with her heels, waiting again for his response to be triggered. But he moved off, obedient to the guiding rein. All around the little grove he carried her, responsive to every signal he received through the reins. It became more and more apparent to her that at one time he had been a well-trained riding horse.

Megan's joy knew no bounds; she felt ready to explode with it. She was right! She had proved herself right! If only she had a saddle. She yearned for a wild gallop. But the little mare's saddle was too small, and she dared not try to get another out here. That would alert Pete for sure. He might already suspect that she spent time with the stallion, too much time in his estimation, but if he ever discovered that she was *riding* him . . . Megan's mouth settled into a grim line. She had no doubt that Pete would forbid her to go near Diablo again. And enforce it by taking away the mare.

Glancing at her watch, she realized that a great deal of time had passed. She had to get back to the ranch. After all, she did have duties there.

She stopped the great horse and slid down without the help of the stump. For a moment she leaned against the barrel of his belly. Her nose was filled with the good warm scent of horseflesh. She rubbed her cheek against him. "You're wonderful," she said soberly. "The most wonderful horse in the world."

He turned his head and nuzzled the seat of her jeans.

Megan laughed. "No nipping now. You'll get your sugar. Here." And she advanced her palm. How could people be afraid of horses? she asked herself as she watched him daintily pick up the sugar. Horses were so great—warm, friendly, solid. They didn't let you down as people sometimes did.

She removed the bridle and gave the stallion a final pat. "You be a good boy now. I'll be back tomorrow." The bridle was repacked in a few minutes, buried deep in the recesses of the saddlebag. Then she swung up onto the mare. Megan smiled. The ground seemed far too close now. She turned the mare homeward.

Pete would be waiting for her, watching and waiting.

She would have to suppress the elation that was surging through her. She felt wonderful. She was on top of the world. She was Bart Dutton's woman. And she had just ridden one of the world's greatest horses.

When she reached the ranch it was approaching lunchtime. She unsaddled the mare and turned her into the corral, then went to hang up her gear. She was coming out of the tack room when Pete appeared.

"Long ride this morning," he said.

Megan tried to look contrite. "I lost track of the time. The prairie's so beautiful. I can hardly believe I spent all those years not realizing how lovely it is."

"Spending an awful lot of time out there, ain't you?" he said dryly.

Megan nodded. She was determined not to let him get a rise out of her. "I guess I do. I guess if you've always lived out here you can't realize what it's like in the city. So many buildings. So many people. So much noise. The prairie's different. It's so peaceful."

Pete looked thoughtful. "Reckon it is. Women don't often take to it, though. Generally they're set on having company." He paused. "Come to think of it, you ain't got any woman friends either."

Megan shrugged. "I've never had many women friends."

Pete chuckled. "Bet they don't know much 'bout horses, huh?"

Megan's laugh rang out. "How did you know, Pete?"

"Don't take much figuring to know what *you* like to talk about. And I figure them Eastern woman ain't much on horses. Leastways, not most of 'em."

"How right you are." Megan had to smile at Pete's whimsical expression.

"Too bad Laina ain't around more. You and her seem to get along well."

"Yes." Megan hoped her expression had not given

her away. "I like her a lot. I suppose she's busy on the circuit all year."

The look Pete gave her was shrewd, but she did not drop her eyes. To do so would surely make him suspicious of her. And she did not want to do that.

"Yep, the circuit keeps 'em pretty busy, all right. But I expect she'll retire one of these days. Make somebody a good wife, she will."

"Yes." Megan could agree to that. "I'm sure she will." She only hoped it wouldn't be Bart!

It wasn't until she was in bed later that Pete's words came back to haunt her. Why weren't Bart and Laina already married? If there was something between them, as Pete implied. How could any woman *put off* marrying Bart? It just didn't make sense. And Bart had said that Laina had nothing to do with what went on between the two of them. Megan wanted to believe him. She had to believe him.

Certainly she didn't wish ill on anyone, least of all Laina, whom she genuinely liked. But Laina had had plenty of time, years, in which to marry Bart. And if she had chosen not to, if she had put her career, or the circuit, or whatever, first, then Megan did not intend to take the blame for the man's loving someone else. *He loves me,* she told herself fiercely as sleep finally overcame her.

He loves me.

Chapter Fifteen

❦

Megan slept hard that night, deeply and soundly. But, as always, her dreams were full of Bart. Bart and Diablo. Once more she was out on the prairie. The sun was just rising—a brilliant kaleidoscope of pink, gold, and orange. She was astride the stallion, having the gallop she had denied herself that morning.

His stride was long and easy, and she clung to him with her legs, relishing the powerful rhythm of him. The wind blew her Stetson off her head, and it hung down her back, flopping there, as her hair flew free behind them. Every cell in her body exulted at the wonder of the horse beneath her, at the glory of being part of him.

The dream faded suddenly and the stallion was gone. She was back with Bart in the motel room in Browning. She could feel his hand cupping her breast, feel the nipple rise against his palm, his kisses in the hollow of her shoulder. She moaned softly. She wanted him so much.

The hand moved down to caress her warm belly.

"Megan." The word was a mere whisper against her ear. "Megan."

The dream was so lovely she didn't want to wake up. But someone was calling her. Bart was calling her, her confused mind said as she struggled toward consciousness. But how could that be? Bart was in the dream.

She opened her eyes slowly. In the dimness of the moonlight she could make out the familiar contours of the room. But the hand was still on her body! And someone was lying beside her.

"Megan love, it's me."

"Bart!" She turned toward him in one swift movement, burrowing against him. "What are you doing here?"

"Ted Rankin came home for an emergency. I hitched a ride. Got to leave again in the morning, though."

"Oh, I'm so glad you waked me." She kissed him thoroughly, coming fully awake in the process. "But you've still got your clothes on."

In the half-light she could see his grin. "Didn't know how you'd react waking up with a naked man in your bed." He chuckled. "You about killed me the night I came to get you for Arabica's labor."

Megan kissed him again. "Silly. That was before." She pushed herself up on one elbow, her fingers reaching for his belt buckle. "That was different." Her hands moved quickly, helping him off with his clothes.

"To tell the truth," he said sheepishly, "I didn't mean to wake you right away. Thought I'd just sleep beside you till you woke up yourself. But I couldn't resist touching you."

"I'm glad," she said simply. "I can *sleep* anytime." Then the rest of what he said registered. "But what about you? You need your sleep."

By this time they had all his clothes off and he was under the covers with her. "I need you more," he replied. "I need you so much it's like a sickness with me." He pulled her into his arms, and she sighed contentedly as their flesh met. "Even up on the broncs I think of you."

"Bart, you mustn't!" Her heart jumped up in her throat at the thought. "You'll get hurt like that."

"Can't help it," he said shortly. "Finally decided I couldn't wait any longer."

Megan kissed his shoulder, left a wet trail of kisses up to his ear, where she circled the lobe lightly with her tongue. "It's only been three days," she said, teasing.

"Seemed like forever to me," he replied, with such heartfelt emotion that she abandoned her raillery.

"Oh, Bart, for me, too."

He pulled her roughly against him, crushing her breasts against his chest. "Listen, woman. I want you. I want you bad. But I've been competing all day and flying half the night. I'm dog-tired—"

"I knew you should sleep," she said, trying to damp her own desire. "Relax and go to sleep now. We'll make love in the morning."

"Dammit," he growled in mock anger. "Don't you ever let a man finish a sentence?"

"Of course I do."

"If you think I can wait till morning, you don't know me very well," he said with a caress that made futile any attempts she might make to put down her own desire. "I was just going to say that I can't make love all night. Like I *want* to. Once now. And once in the morning. Got to be ready for Ted's car at seven. Got to get some sleep in between. Understand?"

"Yes, sir," responded Megan meekly. She got lightly to her knees. "Just lie right there. This won't hurt a bit." And she began to cover his body with feather-light kisses. Beginning with the scar on his forehead and working down over his face to his throat and chest, she caressed him with a multitude of kisses. She lingered over his nipples, flooding with delight as they hardened between her teeth. He smelled so good; her lips tingled from the wiry hair on his chest as her lips passed over it. She caressed him with her mouth, following each scar with a wet pink tongue, until he groaned. "God, woman! You trying to drive me crazy?"

She moved on then, burying her face in his flat belly, kissing his hipbones, trailing her tongue down the outside of one muscular thigh to his knee and then back up the inside. Then she leaned across, her breasts against his leg, to repeat the process on his other thigh, he groaned again. "You're a cruel woman, Megan Ryan." His voice was even deeper than usual. "To tantalize a man like this."

She laughed softly, deep in her throat. She loved him so much. So very much. For a minute longer she teased him, coming near but never quite reaching the part of him she knew yearned most for her touch. When finally she took him in her mouth, his sigh of relief was so heartfelt that she almost giggled.

She had never imagined a love like this—warm, tender, and amusing. It was a revelation to her. As was the fact that she enjoyed taking the initiative. She enjoyed having him, in a very real way, in her power.

His hand came up to touch her breast, to caress the upthrusting nipple. Desire surged within her, making her breath quicken. His other hand moved to the soft skin of her inner thigh. With petal-light strokes he caressed her, moving as she had, closer and closer, yet never quite reaching her most secret place.

She raised her head briefly and looked at him, mischief in her eyes. His gaze met hers and he smiled. That was the only exchange between them, yet when she lowered her head once more his fingers went unerringly to the place that most needed their touch. Ecstasy flooded through Megan, pure, unadulterated ecstasy. And yet she still wanted him. She wanted to be joined to him in the age-old way, as complete a joining of flesh as the human body made possible.

Almost as though he divined her wish, he half rose and pushed her down on her back. His mouth made a quick course from her lips down to each quivering nipple, across the smoothness of her belly, to plant a kiss where she wanted it most. And then he was on his knees, climbing between her legs, and she opened herself to him, her whole body eager for his entrance.

"Ahhhhhhhh!" She could not help the sigh of pure contentment that issued from her as he eased himself into her, as his body came down on hers. "Oh Bart, it's been so long."

"So very long," he agreed, his mouth against her ear, his breath warm on on her throat.

Her fingers clutched spasmodically at the hard muscles of his shoulders as he thrust against her, her body arching wildly upward against his, moving with him, yearning, longing, for that moment of ultimate union that seemed to reach deep into her very soul. She wrapped her arms around him, her hands pressing on his back, holding him tight, tight against her. Her breasts were flattened against the hair of his chest and still she felt the erectness of her nipples pressing into him.

Waves of feeling raced through her. Starting in her loins, they radiated outward, filling her whole body with warmth and joy. Such joy could not be surpassed, she thought. She was his, fully and completely. Bart's woman. She held nothing of herself back. She was his. His now. His forever.

His breath grew more ragged, and hers quickened to match it. Deep within her she felt the first indication of his fulfillment, and her body arched even higher. Quivering with ecstasy, she moved with him, every stroke bringing them closer to the ultimate moment, to the moment when for the barest second in time they could be truly and completely one. And then his breath changed again as he shuddered and, with one last violent stroke, collapsed against her in ecstasy.

She was aware, but only vaguely, of the relaxed weight of his body against hers, as she continued to respond to the waves of ecstasy that swamped her. Finally they receded, leaving her still quivering, every cell aware of the feel of him and yet so completely happy and content that she felt she was floating in pure bliss.

For several minutes they lay as they were, utterly content. Then he rolled over and pulled her close against his side. "What a woman," he sighed. "I'll do you better in the morning, love," he said sleepily. "I'm really beat. Wake me at six. Better set the alarm."

"No need," she said, kissing his chest. "That's when I get up anyway."

His chuckle was heavy with sleep. "An early riser for sure."

She did not reply to this, just snuggling closer against his side, relishing the warmth of him, trying to impress every feeling on her memory for the long lonely nights that would follow this one. Moments later his changed breathing signaled that he slept.

She lay against him for some time, reluctant to lose the feel of him, afraid to move until he was deep in sleep. When finally she did, moving slowly and carefully so as not to wake him, he mumbled, "Stay close," and reached for her. Obediently she shaped herself spoonlike around the hard shape of his back, her breasts against him, her legs entangled in his. "Mmmmm," he muttered, pulling her arm over him as he sank back into slumber.

Megan could not sleep, but she didn't care. She didn't want to miss one second of being close to him. She had never felt more awake, more joyous than she did at the thought that the man sleeping so peacefully beside her had come home for one night, just one night, to be with her. She was so filled with joy that she felt she might explode with it. Surely this meant she had not been wrong about Browning. He felt it, too, felt the bond that existed between them. Toward morning she dozed a little, but the tiny click that meant the alarm was ready to go off roused her, and she raised quickly to one elbow to stop it.

The movement was enough to wake him, so that when she settled back beneath the covers, he had turned and was reaching for her. "Mmmmm," he said, pulling her against him so that their bodies touched each other for their full lengths. "You feel good."

"So do you," she murmured, kissing his throat. "Do you always wake up so quickly?"

"Always," he replied, grinning. "Of course, I don't usually have such good reasons for waking." He buried his face in the valley between her breasts, and she sighed, the desire that had lain dormant through the night leaping immediately into flame. "You lie back this time," he said, looking up at her. "I promise, it won't hurt a bit."

"Yes, doctor," she said, so full of love for him that she felt as if it were oozing out of her pores.

He took a sensitive nipple between his teeth, teasing it as she had his the night before. Megan moved restlessly against him, longing for the feel of his whole body against her own, yet wanting to postpone the moment that meant the end of this time together.

He abandoned her nipple, making long lazy rounds on her breast with his tongue. She reached out blindly, caressing an arm or a leg, whatever part of him she could reach as he covered her breasts with little kisses, then moved across her warm belly.

She knew he was following the pattern she had established the night before, and she sighed. He was going to tease her, tease her and tease her. Restlessly she moved on the bed, unable to lie still under the ministrations of his hands and mouth. He looked up once to grin at her as she moaned in longing, and then he lowered his head to kiss her most secret place.

"Oh, Bart!" The words burst from her. "Darling."

He moved up to her breasts again, and she arched against his mouth, her body surging upward toward his. His lips reached her mouth, teasing and then retreating. She wrapped her arms around his neck and clung to him, her lips on his, her tongue invading his mouth. But his tongue did not retreat. It mingled with hers, sending her even further toward ecstasy.

"God, woman," he said against her neck. "What you do to a man is sinful. Purely sinful."

She pushed him over onto his back and covered his body with her own. "Really?" she teased as she kissed his forehead and moved on to his ears.

"Really," he groaned, his arms binding her tightly to him.

She covered his face with kisses, lingering over his mouth, kissing each corner, running her tongue over his lips. Then she slid slowly down his body, relishing the hard male feel of him against the softness of her breasts, her belly. Every move sending new waves of feeling spilling over her, she continued to go downward until her breasts rested against the fine hair of his legs, and once more she caressed his erect manhood.

Softly, briefly, she caressed him, and then she retraced her way, drawing herself slowly up his body until she reached his lips.

"Oh, Megan," he whispered. "Megan, my love." In one movement he clasped her to him and rolled them both over so that he was on the top.

"Oh, Bart," she whispered. She opened herself automatically for him, but he did not immediately enter her. He raised his head for a moment and looked down on her quizzically. "You feel so good," he said. "Just right against me."

"I know. I feel it, too." She looked up into his eyes, clouded now with desire, and kissed the dark stubble of his beard, moving teasingly to the corner of his mouth.

He shifted suddenly, catching her full on the mouth, crushing her into the bed with all his weight as he kissed her with the full force of his passion.

"Oh, Bart, please," she whispered as he released her lips. "Please, now."

His answer was to enter her. Tenderly, gently, and with a slowness that sent her writhing with impatience, he joined them. Her hips raised of their own accord, her body yearning to make their union complete, to feel him against her.

Then he lowered himself completely, and a tremor shook her as she felt his chest against her sensitive breasts, his manhood deep inside her. She buried her face in the hollow of his shoulder, clung to him with all her might as her body moved in conjunction with his.

The only sound in the room was that of their labored breathing. His arms held her tightly as their passion swept them higher, ever higher. She heard the change in his breathing, felt his convulsive shiver, and her body responded, taking her over the brink at the same time.

They lay together, their breathing gradually slowing to normal. Finally Bart raised his head and looked at the clock. "Got to get up," he said.

She kissed his chin. "I know."

He groaned. "Wish I could stay here." He kissed her forehead. "Like to stay here all day." He grinned. "Right on into the night."

Megan grinned, too. "You'd get hungry."

He shook his head. "I got everything I need right here. Till tomorrow at least." He sighed. "But I've got to go. I've got entry money already paid."

She kissed his neck. "I know. I have work to do, too."

She saw something flicker across his face and added quickly, "Arabica and the filly are doing fine."

"I'm glad." He kissed her nose. "Damn, I wish I didn't have to go."

"Me, too," she said with so much emotion that he grinned again.

He pushed himself up and got to his feet, stooping to pull the covers up around her neck. "Stay put till I'm out of here. You're more than a man can handle."

"Yes, sir." She smiled, letting her eyes drift over his naked body.

"Don't look at me like that," he warned. "I have to go."

"I know. But I can't help it." She grinned. "Women have desires, too, you know."

His answering grin was broad. "I know, baby. But you just stay put. I'll be out of your bathroom and dressed in record time. Then you can have it. Okay?"

"Anything you say, Bart."

He took a step back toward the bed, then stopped himself. "I have to go," he repeated.

With a smile, Megan pulled the sheet up over her head. She heard his hearty laughter as the bathroom door closed behind him.

She lay there, warmed and contented. She would miss him. She would miss him as soon as he walked out that door, but he would be back, back to see her, she told herself with joy.

True to his word, he was out of the bathroom and into his clothes in just a few minutes. He did not come close to the bed. Megan, her head once more uncovered, watched him with love-filled eyes as he tucked his shirt into his jeans and buckled his belt. "I'll be back as soon as I can, love," he said softly. "I hope within a week." He shrugged. "If I can wait that long." His blue eyes flashed at her. "Go back to sleep now. I have a feeling you didn't get much rest last night. Go back to sleep."

Since she knew that was what he wanted, she nodded. "All right, Bart."

He stepped, hand on the doorknob. "Pleasant dreams. And they'd better be of me."

"They always are," she called after him as he closed the door behind him. Some of her good feeling left the room with him, and she struggled with a sudden urge to burst into tears. But that was silly. He had been here. And he would be back. He had promised that.

She sighed and burrowed down under the covers. Her breasts still tingled from the touch of his mouth. Her whole body bore the imprint of his. She was his, fully and completely his. Bart's woman.

Megan closed her eyes and gave herself up to memory until sleep overcame her, and even then she seemed to feel Bart's arms encircling her.

Chapter Sixteen

The days passed slowly, long long days that except for her visits to the stallion were endless and empty. The nights were long, too, nights in which her body clamored for Bart's, clamored for the love it had known so briefly.

The days became a week, and Megan had stopped waiting for a summons to the phone, stopped waiting for a letter. He was busy, she told herself. The rodeo life was a hard one, demanding all a man's attention. To talk to her, to write to her even, would distract him, take his concentration away from the events.

At first she had wondered that Pete had made no mention of Bart's whirlwind visit. Finally it occurred to her that perhaps he did not know. Both Pete and Mrs. Grean were rather late risers. When Bart was not in residence, Megan always breakfasted after her return from the range. And since both also retired rather early and Bart's bed had not been slept in, neither realized he had been there.

Megan hugged the secret of their love to herself, and

whenever ugly doubts raised their heads, as they did
sometimes as the first week grew into a second, she
pushed them firmly down. She was Bart Dutton's
woman, and he would get home to her just as soon as
he could.

The second week had almost drawn to a close and
still there was no word from him. Every morning she
was out early on the west range, riding the great stallion in ever-widening circles around the grove. She had
trotted with him, even taking a little canter. But she
had not yet had that great gallop across the prairie that
she had dreamed of so often. She wanted it, but Bart's
words about prairie-dog holes were burned into her
mind. She couldn't bear it if something happened to
Diablo.

Then she returned from the range one noon to see
Pete wearing a wide grin and whooping. "Hurry up,
girl! Get your fanny offen that horse and help me.
Bart's coming home!"

Megan swung down, her heart in her throat. "Coming home?"

"Yeah. Coming home. For good. He's quitting the
circuit. He done it, Megan! He's retiring!"

Megan, knees suddenly weak, clung to Darling's
saddle. No more competing. No more risking his neck.
He would be here all the time. "When?" she asked
when she could control her voice. "When is he coming?"

"Tonight." In his excitement Pete couldn't stand
still. "Said he had another piece of news fer us, too.
But didn't say what. Man, it'll hafta be good to top
this. I been waiting fer this fer years. Praying, even."

Megan saw the tears in the old man's eyes, tears of
joy.

"What can I do to help?" she said, pushing to the
back of her mind the thought of Bart's "other" news.

Did it have to do with her? With the two of them? She hoped so.

"I don't know." Pete was flustered. "Wait. Here." He thrust a piece of dirty paper at her. "Call these people. Friends. Tell 'em Bart's retiring. We're having a little get-together. Tonight at seven."

"Does Bart know about this party?" she asked.

Pete shook his head. " 'Course not. But he'll enjoy it." The old man's face glowed. "I got to do it, Megan. I got to celebrate. The boss'll understand."

Megan nodded. "Okay, you know him better than I do." She looked down at the list in her hand. "What do the checks mean?"

"I called them already. Couldn't wait to tell some of my old buddies."

Megan smiled. "What about food?"

Pete's grin was wide. "Mrs. Grean'll take care of that. She's already got an oven full of pies. We'll set up the barbecue outside. Nothing to worry about there. Just let them people know."

"I will," Megan replied. "As soon as I take care of Darling."

"I'll get one of the boys to do that. You get on the phone."

"Okay." Megan turned toward the house. Her heart was still pounding, her knees still weak, as she tried to assimilate the news. She could hardly believe that Bart would no longer be risking his neck on saddle broncs, that he would be here, here on the Rocking D all the time. It was too wonderful to take in at once.

She pushed open the kitchen door, to have her nostrils assailed by the smell of baking pies. She sniffed appreciatively—apple, cherry, berry. "Mrs. Grean! They smell just wonderful."

The housekeeper looked up from where she was busy rolling out more crusts. "It's the most wonderful

news since Mr. Bart's first world championship," she
said, her round face aglow. "We all been worried about
him, you know. A man shouldn't be pushing his luck
forever. Too many broken bones can cause problems."
She laughed heartily. "I never seen a man who hated
being laid up more than Mr. Bart. Lucky thing he
didn't have a wife.˙ Poor thing would have been pure
crazy with the man carrying on like that. Won't be no
more of that, thank the good Lord."

Megan nodded. "Pete gave me a list of people to
call. Guests for the party."

Mrs. Grean nodded. "Whyn't you use the phone
right over there, child? All the folks around'll be glad
of the news. Mr. Bart's real popular."

"Yes, I'm sure he is." Megan settled herself on a
chair and reached for the phone.

Almost an hour later she put down the phone and
shrugged weary shoulders.

"Got them all?" asked the housekeeper.

"Yes. Every last one. And almost all of them said
they'd be here." Megan smiled. "Bart will be surprised."

Mrs. Grean eyed her shrewdly. "Said he had a surprise for us. Wonder what it is."

Megan shrugged. "I haven't any idea," she said,
willing herself to keep her expression serene.

Mrs. Grean glanced at her watch. "My, my, it's getting on. If you haven't anything else pressing, could
you run a dust rag over the furniture for me?"

"Of course, Mrs. Grean." Megan's grin was genuine.
"Is there anything else I can do?"

The housekeeper hesitated for a moment. "Well, I
hate to ask it of you, but with these pies and all . . ."

"Come on, Mrs. Grean, I'm glad to do anything."

"Well, if you'd just change the sheets on Mr. Bart's

bed. I always do when he's coming home. There's something special about fresh sheets, you know."

"Of course, Mrs. Grean. I'll do that first." Megan turned toward the stairs so the housekeeper couldn't see her face.

"You'll find the sheets in the linen closet in the hall," the housekeeper called after her.

"Yes, Mrs. Grean," Megan called back over her shoulder, a smile breaking out on her face. She would have to remind Bart to mess up his bed before Mrs. Grean got up in the morning. Her smile broadened. She was fairly certain he wouldn't be sleeping in it tonight.

As she moved around changing the linen, she considered his room. It was a plain room, completely unadorned, nothing in it to mark it as Bart's. On an impulse she opened the closet door and buried her face in one of his shirts. Tonight, this very night, he would be back! She pulled back and shut the door quickly. What on earth would Mrs. Grean think if she found her like that!

Megan stripped the bed and put on the fresh linen, pulling each corner tight. Then she stood back, admiring the job. Someday she would make their bed every morning. She pulled back. Thoughts like that could be dangerous, she warned herself. Hadn't she resolved not to rush things, to be content to be Bart's woman?

But what could Bart's news be? She made a face at herself in the mirror and gathered up the old bedclothes, carrying them downstairs as she went to get the dust cloth.

By six o'clock Mrs. Grean had everything under control. The house was spotless. Several hands, under the supervision of a glowing Pete, had the barbecue going. And Megan had been sent off to her room to get herself ready.

In just an hour he would be home, she told herself

as she stepped into the shower. Home for good. And tonight they would be together. Her whole body grew heated at the thought. It might be late, of course, by the time the guests had gone. But she had no doubt that sometime tonight Bart would come to her bed. And then . . .

She hurried out of the shower and toweled herself briskly. No time to think about such things now. She had to get dressed. She slipped into a fresh shirt and jeans and brushed her hair vigorously. How she longed for his touch. She pulled on her boots and hurried down the stairs and outside. She wanted to be the first to see him.

But she was to be disappointed in that. The yard was already full of chattering cowhands, all of them with eyes that kept going toward the main road. Megan joined them, drifting aimlessly here and there, not hearing a word that was said to her.

The approaching car was seen by almost all of them at once, and a shout went up. Pete came racing out of the kitchen. "That's the Darwood car," he said. "Wonder if they got Bart with them."

Megan caught her breath. She had not called the Darwoods, had not even thought of them. As the car came slowly up the lane, her heart began to pound in her throat and her knees went weak. He was here. She heard the shout that told he'd been seen.

She would have remained in the background as Pete and the others surged forward, but their rush carried her partway to the car. So it was that she had a clear view of Bart getting out of the car, of him turning to extend his hand to someone inside. Megan saw the hand that reached out to take his, saw the diamond on it glittering in the sunlight. She watched Laina Darwood emerge and smile at Pete. "Congratulate me, you old devil," she said. "I've got my man at last."

Waves of hot and cold washed over Megan as the cowhands surged around to ask Bart a hundred questions. So this was why he had kept his visit home a secret. He hadn't wanted Laina to hear about it.

Megan wasn't quite sure how she got there, but she found herself in the stable, saddling the mare. She led her out the back way. The stable was between them and the yard. It wasn't likely anyone would see them go. And if they did, it didn't matter. Her presence wasn't needed at the party. It was Bart's party, Bart's and Laina's. She urged the mare into a canter. That was his other news. Laina had decided not to wait any longer.

A dry sob wrenched in Megan's throat. How could she have been such a fool? Bart's woman, indeed. She was only an amusement, someone to play around with while he waited for Laina to make up her mind.

Megan bit her lip to keep back the tears. She would have to go back to the ranch eventually. She would have to face them all and offer Laina and Bart her congratulations. But she couldn't do it just yet. She needed time. Time to kill her dreams, she thought drearily. Time to realize that she had never had a chance. She would leave the Rocking D tomorrow. She knew that with certainty. She could not bear to be around Bart after this.

But there was one dream she could still realize. Tonight she would ride the great stallion. He knew the prairie. It was his home. He wasn't likely to step into a prairie-dog hole. And if he did—perhaps a broken neck would hurt less than a broken heart.

The mare had reached the clump of cottonwoods, and Megan looked around eagerly. She had not come out in the evening often. What if Diablo wasn't here? But she heard his welcoming nicker from the other side of the creek, and by the time he arrived she had the bridle out of the saddlebag. It was a matter of moments to slip it on him. Then he went of his own accord to the stump that she used to mount him.

In spite of her heartache, she smiled. "We're going to have a ride tonight, boy. A great ride." The smile faded. "One to last a lifetime."

She got up on the stump and swung herself astride, then urged him out from under the trees. The sun was low in the west, its rays painting the sky in vivid hues. She turned her back to it.

She didn't know if Diablo used his eyes to avoid dangers, but she, at least, could see better with the sun at her back. She put the horse into a walk, her knees tightening against his sides. First she wanted to do a little more thinking. Then they would have their run. "I don't understand how he could do this to me," she told the horse. "I thought he loved me."

He never said so, a voice in her head reminded her. *He never said that at all.*

"But he let me believe—"

The more fool you, reiterated the voice. *You fell for him like some stupid rodeo groupie.*

The tears stung Megan's eyes. "Oh, Diablo," she sobbed. "I should have stuck to horses. They don't let you down."

"Megan! Wait!" The call came clearly across the silent prairie. She raised her head in surprise and saw the approaching horseman. "Megan! Please!"

Sheer panic overtook her then. She could not face him, could not listen to his excuses. All she could think of was getting away. She wheeled the stallion. "Now, boy. Go!"

The great horse needed no second command. He took off with a bound that almost unseated her, but she clung to him, hands tangled in his mane. To her grief-stricken mind the stallion was her salvation. He would carry her away, far away where Bart couldn't reach her. Beyond that, her numbed reasoning could not go.

"Megan! No! Don't run him! Wait! Please, wait!" The sound of pursuing hooves came to her as he urged his horse in pursuit.

She laughed wildly. No horse could catch Diablo. No horse alive. Let Bart follow them as long as he pleased. Diablo could outrun anything on the Rocking D, anything in Montana.

The wind whipped her hair about and it stung her eyes, but she didn't care. She didn't care about anything but escaping from Bart.

Suddenly she was conscious that the sounds of pursuit had stopped. Throwing a glance over her shoulder, she saw that Bart's horse was standing still some distance away. He was standing still, and he was riderless. She could just make out Bart's motionless form beside him on the ground.

"Bart!" The cry sprang from her lips unbidden as she wheeled the great stallion and sped back toward them. She stopped Diablo some distance away and slid hurriedly to the ground. For a moment she was afraid her legs wouldn't carry her, but then they moved and she ran across the prairie to drop to her knees beside him.

"Bart! Oh, Bart! Are you hurt?" She tried to examine his silent form. He was lying sprawled on his back. She couldn't see any blood. She stroked his head absently as she tried to decide what to do. It was growing dark. If she left him out here on the prairie, how would they find him again? But what if he was so seriously injured that he needed medical aid? If she rode Diablo, she might get to the ranch and lead them back before complete darkness fell. She half rose to her knees. That was what she would do. Almost without thinking, she bent to drop a gentle kiss on his forehead, but as she straightened a hard hand encircled her wrist.

Relief washed over her in great waves. "Bart, are you all right? What happened?"

"I want to talk to you."

"You've been injured," she said, forgetting everything else in her desire to take care of him. "I've got to go get help."

"No, Megan." He sat up. "I'm not hurt. Not at all. I wasn't thrown."

"But why—I don't understand." She stared at him in confusion.

"I stopped the horse and lay down on the prairie," he said calmly, but his hold on her wrist tightened. "I knew you wouldn't ride off and let me lie."

"Oh!" She strained against his grip, trying to release her wrist, to get away from him.

"You wouldn't stop," he reminded her. "Not only that—I was afraid you'd kill yourself on that horse."

"Let me go!" she cried. "Let me go!"

He shook his head. "Nothing doing. I want some explanations."

Megan could hardly believe her ears. "You've come to the wrong person," she cried.

"I don't think so. How long have you been riding him?" His gesture indicated the stallion.

"Two or three weeks," she answered defiantly.

"Against my direct orders." His mouth grew grim.

"You were wrong about him," Megan said, prying futilely at his fingers. "He's not a killer."

"He might have thrown you, stomped you."

"He didn't. Let me go." She avoided his eyes. "I admit I was wrong to disobey you. So fire me. I don't care." What difference did it make? She was leaving anyway the first chance she got.

"That isn't all," he said, his eyebrows almost

touching from the ferocity of his frown. "I want to know why you ran out on my party."

Megan stared at him. Had he really expected her to stay there and celebrate his engagement to Laina?

"I thought you wanted me to quit the circuit," he continued, his eyes boring into hers.

"I—I did think it was dangerous," she admitted.

"Then why didn't you stay to celebrate?"

"I—" She couldn't hold back the tears any longer. They spilled down her cheeks. "I didn't want to hear your special news."

It was his turn to stare at her. "Didn't want to?"

"No," she continued. "I don't see why you wanted me there anyway."

He gazed at her in perplexity. "Do you love me?" he asked, his eyes on her face.

"Of course not!" Why must he make it so difficult? Couldn't he let her keep her pride at least? "We enjoyed each other. That's all it was. A little fun."

To her surprise his face grew even grimmer. "A little fun," he repeated harshly. "And I suppose if you didn't feel like some 'fun,' I wouldn't mean a thing to you."

"Exactly." The lie stuck in her throat, but she forced it out.

"We'll see about that," he cried and with a quick movement thrust her down on her back in the grass and threw himself on top of her.

"Let me go," she cried, beating at him with her fists.

"Shut up! I'm going to try a little experiment." And his mouth descended on hers. She tried to avoid it, twisting her head desperately, but he buried his hands in her hair and held her head immobile. She tried, she tried as hard as she could, to stay cold, not to respond. But she loved him, in spite of everything she loved him. And gradually her lips softened and opened under his.

"Now," he said when at last he raised his head. "Tell me you don't love me."

"How can you be so cruel?" She stared up at him from tear-filled eyes. "Why can't you just let me be? Go back to your party. Go back to Laina."

"To Laina?" he said in puzzlement. "What's she got to do with this?"

"I told you," she sobbed. "I know your news. I saw the ring. I know she's finally decided to marry you."

Her eyes were blinded by her tears and so she could not see his face, but to her amazement she heard him burst into laughter. "So that's what this is all about," he said. "Megan, I'm not going to marry Laina."

"But—but I saw the ring! I heard her."

"She was telling Pete her good news. She finally got a proposal out of the bulldogger she's loved since high school."

"But Pete said . . ."

Bart frowned. "That old matchmaker evidently thought a little jealousy would help things along."

"You mean you and Laina were never—"

"Never anything but friends," he said. "And my other news had nothing to do with her."

She was suddenly very conscious of his body on hers. "It didn't?"

"No, it didn't. It had to do with us."

"Oh." She waited, holding her breath.

"I came home to ask you to marry me," he said. "*That's* why I quit the circuit. Because I can't stand being away from you." He grinned ruefully. "A man my age can't be making love all night and riding broncs all day. Something's got to give." He kissed the tip of her nose. "If I let you up, will you promise not to run away?"

"I promise," she whispered.

"Good." He started to raise himself, then stopped.

"You will marry me, won't you? We've got a whole ranchful of people back there waiting for an announcement."

"Yes," she said. "I'll marry you. And Bart . . ." She put her arms around his neck. "I'm sorry about Diablo. You've got every right to be mad at me. Pete told me you'd be really angry. I didn't mean to make you look bad by taming him. Only I believe in him and I had to do it."

"You realize, of course, that all the neighboring ranchers will be laughing at me," he said, eyeing her now with a strange expression. "A little bit of a thing like you riding *him*."

"Oh, Bart, I'm sorry! I . . ." She forced herself to say it. "I won't ride him."

Again his laughter rang out across the prairie. "You don't know me as well as you think," he said, grinning down at her. "When I saw you in the stall with him, I thought sure you'd be killed. I was afraid for you." He brushed her lips with a kiss.

"But Pete said . . ."

He shook his head. "Pete's an interfering old geezer, and I mean to tell him so. Do you think I'm so small a man that I can't let my woman succeed?"

She shook her head.

"The truth of the matter is that every man in the county is going to envy me my beautiful red-haired wife who delivers colts and rides a former mankiller. Why, when they see you on that stallion and know you're *my* woman . . ." His smile spread from ear to ear. "Every man jack of them will wish they could trade places with me."

"But I'll always belong to you," she said softly.

"You'd better," he said fiercely and kissed her with deep passion. Then he raised his head and glanced up at the sky. "Come on, woman. We can't keep our guests waiting much longer. Get the bridle off that pet dog of yours and we'll head back to our guests."

He got up and helped her to her feet. Megan moved toward the stallion. He was shifting nervously, but he stood for her. She pulled off the bridle and he whirled away, snorting before he took off across the prairie, tail in the air.

"Darling's hitched at the grove ahead," she said.

He nodded as he swung up on the roan. "Come on up here and we'll go get her. But you've got to behave yourself," he said as he reached a hand down to help her up and settled her on the saddle in front of him. "Because we can't expect our guests to wait *all* night."

"I'll be good," she promised, twisting to give him a peck on the cheek. "After all, the quicker we get back and tell them, the quicker the party will be over."

"I read you," he chuckled, his breath against her ear. "The quicker *that* party is over, the quicker our private one can begin."

"You put things so nicely," she sighed as she snuggled back against him. "But I'm not really sure if I should marry you."

"And why not?" he demanded.

"You made me confess to loving you, but you never—"

"I love you, Megan Ryan. I love you madly, wildly, completely."

"And I love you." In spite of her promise, she twisted once more to kiss him. She was Bart Dutton's woman. Now. And forever.

RAPTURE ROMANCE—*Reader's Opinion Questionnaire*

Thank you for filling out our questionnaire. Your response to the following questions will help us to bring you more and better books, by telling us what you are like, what you look for in a romance, and how we can best keep you informed about our books. Your opinions are important to us, and we appreciate your help.

1. What made you choose this particular book? (This book is #_____)
   Art on the front cover_____
   Plot descriptions on the back cover_____
   Friend's recommendation_____
   Other (please specify)_____

2. Would you rate this book:
   Excellent_____
   Very good_____
   Good_____
   Fair_____

3. Were the love scenes (circle answers):
   A. Too explicit   Not explicit enough   Just right
   B. Too frequent   Not frequent enough   Just right

4. How many Rapture Romances have you read?

5. Number, from most favorite to least favorite, romance lines you enjoy:
   Adventures in Love_____
   Ballantine Love and Life_____
   Bantam Circle of Love_____
   Dell Candlelight _____
   Dell Candlelight Ecstasy_____
   Jove Second Chance at Love_____
   Harlequin_____
   Harlequin Presents_____
   Harlequin Super Romance_____
   Rapture Romance_____
   Silhouette_____
   Silhouette Desire_____
   Silhouette Special Edition_____

6. Please check the *types* of romances you enjoy:
   Historical romance_____
   Regency romance_____
   Romantic suspense_____
   Short, light contemporary romance_____
   Short, sensual contemporary romance_____
   Longer contemporary romance_____

7. What is the age of the oldest _____ youngest _____ heroine you would like to read about? The oldest _____ youngest _____ hero?

8. What elements do you dislike in a romance?
   Mystery/suspense_____
   Supernatural_____
   Other (please specify) _____

9. We would like to know:
   ● How much television you watch
      Over 4 hours a day_____
      2–4 hours a day_____
      0–2 hours a day_____
   ● What your favorite programs are
      _____
      _____
   ● When you usually watch television
      8 a.m. to 5 p.m._____
      5 p.m. to 11 p.m._____
      11 p.m. to 2 a.m._____

10. How many magazines do you read regularly?
   More than 6_____
   3–6_____
   0–3_____
   Which of these are your favorites?
   _____
   _____

To get a picture of our readers, and to know where to reach them, the following personal information will be most helpful, if you don't mind giving it, and will be kept only for our records.

Name _____
Address_____
City _____
State_____ Zip code_____

Please check your age group:
   17 and under_____
   18–34_____
   35–49_____
   50–64_____
   64 and older_____

Education:
   Now in high school_____
   Now in college_____
   Graduated from high school_____
   Completed some college_____
   Graduated from college_____

Are you now working outside the home?
   Yes_____ No_____
   Full time_____
   Part time_____
   Job title_____

Thank you for your time and effort. Please send the completed questionnaire and answer sheet to: Robin Grunder, RAPTURE ROMANCE, New American Library, 1633 Broadway, New York, NY 10019